Julia Sherman Hallock

Broken Notes from a Gray Nunnery

Julia Sherman Hallock

Broken Notes from a Gray Nunnery

ISBN/EAN: 9783743338197

Manufactured in Europe, USA, Canada, Australia, Japa

Cover: Foto ©Andreas Hilbeck / pixelio.de

Manufactured and distributed by brebook publishing software
(www.brebook.com)

Julia Sherman Hallock

Broken Notes from a Gray Nunnery

BROKEN NOTES

FROM

A GRAY NUNNERY

BY

JULIA SHERMAN HALLOCK

BOSTON
LEE AND SHEPARD PUBLISHERS
10 MILK STREET
1896

TO

MRS. L. B. MORRIS

THIS LITTLE BOOK IS AFFECTIONATELY
INSCRIBED

JULIA SHERMAN HALLOCK

CONTENTS

BROKEN NOTES FROM A GRAY NUNNERY

JANUARY.

This first day of the year has been gloriously wild and dark, filled with the exultant rush and roar of a driving rain.

We had our tea early, Phyllis and I, and I hoped for a song or a hymn with the old melodeon for accompaniment, when the day's work was done and our firelight had begun its twilight dance with the shadows; but instead, she read in silence while I lolled lazily in my pet rocker, too lulled and satisfied to care for books, while listening to that "strife more sweet than peace," as it rose and fell and rose again, outside.

Phyllis, with lids downcast and lips full of repose, made an enchanting picture, sitting so quietly with the shaded lamplight soft on her bright hair and a reflected glow from the red-covered table on which she leaned, deepening her own marvellous coloring, till I thought, if one wished for a living symbol of June, here she is with her roses!

And yet Phyllis is no longer young, only as the austere pleasures of simple living, with wholesome habits and pure thoughts, have kept her so.

I have been thinking, too, of that blessed day which brought me a letter from Phyllis. I was lingering in the city, amid uncongenial surroundings, and although my work from its sheer wearisomeness brought soundest sleep at night and left little scope for sentiment by day, I was continually dreaming of the country, with a deep and homesick longing to go back and live once more among my native rocks. Phyllis had always lived among them, but she was now living absolutely alone, except for Dandy Jim, her pet cat, and her letter said, "Come!" At that word the fetters seemed to drop from my soul, and I turned my face homeward with the heart of a pilgrim, whose shrine and Mecca are in the past.

I like to recall the stormy winter day, fast waning, when, after a slow drive from the station, I reached the home end of the long lane that turns in from the narrow street, and was set down by the wide stone steps leading toward the steep yard in front of the gray old house.

Phyllis stood in the open doorway, the radiance of

her self-forgetful welcome made so pathetic by the deep mourning dress she wore and the traces of grief in her face, that for a remorseful moment I was quite ashamed to have been so glad in my eagerness to fill a vacancy lately made by death.

But when after our long evening talk I retired to my pleasant south chamber, and sank into the downy deeps of an old-fashioned bed, I thought I had never before known genuine repose. How still the rooms were! How wide and free the storm-swept waste outside! All night, at intervals, the wind, like a friendly watchman, came down from the cedar-sentinelled hills to gently shake the doors and windows and steal away with a long-drawn "all's well!" soothing as any cradle-song to drowsy ears. The town I had left seemed thousands of miles away.

Since then the months have come and gone, and I am still greedy over these uneventful days of mine, whose untainted silences, so rich with sky and sun and storm, leave the ear and the soul free to listen and adore. In their midst we too live our own intense lives, and are never dull, although we are sometimes feelingly commiserated by the uninitiated, on account of our isolation and limited resources. And then we wax argumentative and ask, Is not all creation full of echoes? It was no less a personage than Emerson who said, "The blue zenith is the point in which romance and reality meet." Have we not all the room betwixt earth and sky to grow up in, and if we remain puny and undeveloped here, might we not elsewhere? Besides, we have learned that "a handful with quietness is better than both hands full with vexation."

One day, half in love and half in fun, we christened our habitation "The Nunnery." The new name has clung to it, and the more we use it the fitter it seems. For although we have not shorn our locks, nor taken the veil, neither formal vows, the "pomps and vanities" of life do not concern us, and we realize fully that very near domestic ties and high social ambitions are not for us, while we dare believe that much, perhaps the best, remains. Is not this, in a measure, the true "nun" spirit?

JANUARY 2.

Yesterday's down-pour left scarcely a hint of snow. The bare earth lies richly brown in the sunshine. The brook in our lane boils under its wooden roof, and joyfully escapes to spread out over the gray sedge, wide and shining and full of peace.

EVENING.

A tempestuous snow-squall has turned our corner of the world hoary again, adding, by contrast, to the sheltered warmth of our ingle-side.

Phyllis has been diligently sewing, while I have read aloud.

JANUARY 6.

What can be more beautiful than snow in the country, with its unsullied spaces lying so fair under the open sky? The storm began yesterday. From my chamber window it was a delight to watch the swarming of the " wild, white bees." They recalled some lines I read when a child.

> " The far-off mountain's misty form
> Is entering now a tent of storm,
> And all the valley is shut in
> By flickering curtains, gray and thin."

That verse always made an exquisite picture in my mind.

The snowfall has continued fitfully until this afternoon. It is light and dry, for the air is very cold, and we have had an easy time with our snow-shovels. Phyllis made a picturesque figure in her black coat and gown, and broad soft hat, tied "poke" wise under her rosy chin. The sunset clouds were brilliant with orange and crimson. In their light the dried leaves clinging to the oaks on the eastern hill glowed golden red, quiver-

ing like little flames when the wind touched them. We
always love their sonorous whispering.

The extreme cold continues. Even the oldest in-
habitant on our country-side freely admits we are in
the toils of an old-fashioned winter. The one road in
sight of our windows is blockaded most of the time.

There a r e d a y s to-
gether, when neither
horses nor men come
this way. As for our
neighbors, they are all
too far off to even
show us the smoke
from their chimneys. Nevertheless "two bugs in
one rug" were never more snug than Phyllis and
I.   What could be pleasanter than this same long,
brown kitchen, softly lighted from the southern and
western sky! It is cosily warm, and swept and
dusted, for Phyllis believes that "neatness is the ele-
gance of poverty," and come rich or poor, her imme-
diate surroundings must always be elegant.   Books
and work are within easy reach.   Dandy Jim stretches
his glossy black and white length luxuriously in
the biggest and softest chair, while sleeping off the
effects of last night's dissipation.   The wood fire glows
and leaps responsive to every gusty breath in the huge

chimney, and the steamy strain of our round black kettle sets one dreaming of waterfalls in the woods of spring, or the humming of bees in the apple-blooms. Outside, in the " nipping and eager air," are the chick-adees. They are glad to come countless times in a day to our back windows, where Phyllis always keeps some tidbit for them. What delicate creatures they are, yet so gay and plucky, no matter how cold and un-friendly the cold blast may be! They are sweet and living sermons, and seem to exhort the over-anxious heart to be fearlessly glad in to-day, and as fearlessly trustful for to-morrow.

JANUARY 14.

Bitterly cold. This morning our well was actually frozen over! Nevertheless, at noon when I went out for a few minutes, I thought how perfect the winter day. Not a sound was there, except now and then a bird-note, for the winds were hushed and the trees as still as a picture. The woods and hills, shimmering through silvery gossamer, looked remote and mystical, like some City of God. Under the celestial paleness of the sky the rigid earth's white face shone glorified. It was as if Divine Love looked on Death and smiled. This evening Phyllis and I have been making charcoal sketches of each other. It was great sport. She has gone to dreamland now, and is taking her beauty sleep, which I shall not, for it is past eleven.

A bird flew into my room to-day and fluttered about in an agony of fright. I lowered a window opposite the one by which he entered and he darted for it instantly,

but alighted for a moment on the edge of the sash and uttered two or three little notes of triumph, or thanks, before flying away.

JANUARY 14.

The early morning was exquisite with frost. The well's " breath " became visible in shapes of impalpable gray. The bucket and inner sides of the curb were shaggy with a crystallized mimicry of moss and fern, as fantastic as it was evanescent, while the real mosses and ferns were grizzled and hoar, like an old man's beard.

At twilight there was the daintiest of new moons, — " a silver shallop " on an opaline sea.

We have milder airs, but are still cut off from walks beyond our private domain. Plenty of exercise and fresh air the well-being of my soul demands always. So now, when we get short of snow paths, and I am in sore need of calisthenics, I go to the back yard and carry the wood-pile to cover. The sticks, being of green oak, are as solid as one could wish, and I can manage but a small basketful at a time; but there is joy in its fresh, woodsy odor, and the contact of the rough and richly covered bark, with its lichens and beard-like tufts of olive gray: a sort of speech they seem, of the " incommunicable trees."

I am thinking to-night of one dreary year, when I had less patience, perhaps, than now. Physical ills kept me in close confinement, and I felt unutterably withered. The days followed each other in such dull fashion, that when I looked back and tried to separate them I was unable to do so. They were born with blank eyes and leaden faces, and went down to their death with no change of expression. Then how I dreamed of God's fathomless skies, of his  mountains towering sunward, of his wind-swept plains and shadowy woods and full-voiced rivers! Feverish

visions swept by such tempests of tears and longing,
as caused me to wonder if I were not cursed with
gypsy-blood, that houses and "folks" and their end-
less train of small ambitions should be to me such a
weariness. In my heart I must always keep a great
pity for all prisoners.

JANUARY 23.

Dark and damp and sullenly cold. The fires are too
lifeless to give much comfort. Phyllis asked me to-day
if I thought this winter would prove to be "the winter
of our discontent;" then she smiled brightly and went
to feed the birds. The sparrows are here now — little
red-heads, with all the choleric temper usually credited
to red-heads. Their fracases with one another are
amusing, their motto, evidently, like that of the human
race is, "Each one for himself and the devil catch the
hindmost!" Phyllis scatters oatmeal and crumbs for
these, and they evidently prefer it to a meat diet, in
spite of the theory that "gentle manners are cultivated
by a diet of cereals," and *vice versa*. Deep inroads are
made, however, on chickadees' supply of fresh suet by
the woodpecker. Practical, hard-headed forager, with
a bright eye out for business, no airs, no caprices, unless
it be sometimes in the tree, when he appears to be play-
ing peek-a-boo. The only bit of poetry about him is the
knot of scarlet velvet at the back of his black and
white cap ; but he is not domineering, and the chicks are

not afraid of him, only a little anxious, I fancy, over his appallingly persistent appetite.

The sparrow, though bold and cheeky, appears suspicious of human kind; the chickadee shows a most willing and cheerful confidence in our good-will; but the woodpecker seems quite indifferent to us, caring for nothing, literally, but his grub. Dandy Jim sits on the window-sill, and watches them with a benign and fatherly air, and knows as well as we that they are members of our family and not subjects for prey.

JANUARY 31.

Within doors this evening I felt so heated and breathless that I went out and sat for a while on the stone steps. I could look up through a tangle of crooked boughs, dim against cloud draperies that half shone from the full moon behind them. How serene and patient the world looked in that quiet light and air! I think my heart prayed, though my lips found no words.

FEBRUARY.

FEBRUARY 4.

Savagely cold again, but grand in its splendors of white light and steely sky. One needs faith to see any love or brooding care in those rarefied deeps. A glittering snow-crust stretches bleakly away on all sides of our nunnery, and the swaying woods are full of deep tones. The gale is so powerful I can almost fancy it makes the starbeams flicker.

A sense of sublimity fails, however, to keep flesh and
blood warm, and we are prone to hug the stove, and in
danger of becoming grovelling fire-worshippers. On
such a night we do not scorn the company of two hot
soapstones apiece in our twin snow-banks of beds, and
often think of an old woman who, when we were
children, lived here all alone. She inhabited the north
room mostly, and for that reason, perhaps, formed the
habit of wearing her bonnet all the time, and of sleeping
between two feather-beds, without removing any of her
clothing, not even her shoes! But we give her our
tender and intelligent sympathy, and realize that if we
were not joined to our idols, and hopelessly infatuated
with home privacy and personal freedom, we should be
tempted to acknowledge ourselves uncomfortable.

FEBRUARY 7.

The snow is fast melting. The brook that last week
crept in muffled darkness between its white curved
borders, lifts its swelling bosom to the sun, and chants
its little chant to life and liberty.

Rabbit tracks — "Bunny's autograph" Gibson calls
them — in snow on the bank before our front windows.
Depressions in snow on north side of bars, where the sunlight has shone between them.

Phyllis has been out for a long walk and a call on a
neighbor, who sent me from her furnace-heated house a
nosegay of flowers, their delicate beauty enhanced by

green and white foliage. Their perfume is not more
real or penetrating than the memories they bring.
" Their soft leaves wound me with a
grief whose balsam never grew."

How impossible to leave the things
that are behind! They are a part of
one's very self, even though they may
belong to a foolish time, when we dared
to see visions and dream dreams in the
face of a world full of ghastly meanings
and grim fatalities. " For O, at that
age, when it seems as if we could never
die, how deathless, how flushed and
mighty, as with the youngness of a god,
is all that our hearts create ! "

I never yet thanked God that I was not so badly off
as some others, nor did it ever solace me to think so, for
I never have been so glad or so sad that my ear forgot
to hearken to that "perpetual wail, as of souls in pain,"
that continually ascended from this burdened world.

Ah, to be able to fear nothing, — to believe unfal-
teringly that " we cannot escape from our good," no
matter in what strange garb it may walk with us ! There
are moments when we feel sure ; and while the angel
tarries, the army of pigmies that would enslave us for-
gets its cunning. Then, indeed, it does not matter
whether one governs a kingdom or sweeps a crossing,
nor even if one is but a voiceless little reed that, long
ago, the gods left desolate in the lowlands.

FEBRUARY 18.

This morning we awoke to the biggest snow-storm of the season. Our well was lined with cushions of downy white, and so nearly closed in, a few feet from the water, that it looked like a mammoth hanging nest. We have tried to keep the back steps cleared for the sake of our birds. When the stones were just filmed over, the slender feet made such delicate traceries, — embroidered muslin and diaphanous lace draperies could not be daintier. The sky is still overcast, but at sunset the west was faintly suffused with a vague rose-tint from the ruddy embers burning behind the clouds — a rare background of color for pearl and gray branches. Between us and the untravelled road lie drifts that would discourage anything short of an ox-sled or a snow-plough.

I have been reading Balzac's " Cæsar Birotteau." My mind (or my lack of it) is confused by the innumerable characters, and their legal (and illegal) transactions with each other. " 'Tis a' a muddle," but the feeling is exquisite. and I am constantly adoring the writer's genius. his delicate sensibility and masterful strength in portraying human nature.

FEBRUARY 20.

The nearest approach to a blizzard came this morning, and was perfectly furious while it lasted. The fine snow sifted through every unguarded crevice, and left miniature pyramids and mountain ranges in all sorts of unlooked-for places. Now, at 4 P.M., the clouds are gone, and the sky is pale and clear — infinitely spiritual, but O, so far off and cold! The dazzling packed banks and sharp-edged drifts, with their shadows of atmospheric blue, look marbleized.

The birds still come in gay and greedy flocks of ten or twenty. Their sweet notes relieve the bleakness of the air, and make the longed-for coming of spring seem nearer.

In the height of the storm a large soft-breasted bird from the woods, a pigeon probably, flew into our porch, as if for protection. He appeared bewildered and exhausted. Phyllis threw out a generous piece of bread, but he failed to interpret her good-will, though he lingered near for some time after. We hope the beautiful stranger may not perish from cold or famine before this bitter winter is over.

I have been out but once, and then because we had to open the paths, which in some places had drifted waist-high. The gale puffed our skirts until we looked like animated balloons, and our faces felt as if they were freezing, but there was a sense of exultation in our tussle that set the blood dancing. I hope when I die it may be with my " boots on " and in some convulsion of nature.

We are quite cut off from communication with our kind, and know the full meaning of " twelve miles from a lemon," for the grocer's clerk does not come; we are out of kerosene and have no candles. This afternoon Phyllis has improvised a "poverty lamp" that we view  with some lugubrious mirth. A sauce-plate filled with cottolene, in which a shoestring is disposed, with its two ends hanging out to await the inspiration of a match. As a burlesque on the little antique Roman lamp, it is an undoubted success. Phyllis suggests that we set it under the kitchen glass to burn before vanity's shrine; as women generally are supposed to worship there.

FEBRUARY 28.

The earth is heavily banked with snow, the surface of which is covered with dimples; little irregular depressions, and long, wavy lines like winrows or tide marks. The eaves drip silver rain in the sunshine. I can hear the big drops beating on a tin vessel outside. They sound like a distant cow-bell, and make a plaintive monotone that produces melancholy, from some vague association, probably.

Every sound brings with it the echo of some other, and with that a something else, subtler than any sound. I think it is the spirit of things. Pools of snow water stand on the stone flagging, and black puddles shine wherever the earth is bare.

EVENING.

This afternoon, a little before sunset, softened rays streamed through the cloud curtains of g r a y i s h gold, and illumined the woods on the western slope. The oak-leaves are losing somewhat of their russet color a n d leathery texture. In a strong light they appear half-transparent. Faithful friends of the win-  ter woods, their final scattering on the late snowfields is not without pathos.

MARCH.

MARCH 1.

We have had a call to-day from a motherly woman, who came in company with her big dog. Her only and idolized son has recently left home, and she is so lonely that she came away to escape her thoughts. When she does sit down and give way to tears, Tige comes and lays his noble head in her lap and licks her hands and looks at her with a world of tender trouble in his great brown eyes. What human could do more?

Blessed is the grief that may be told! There is all the difference between that and the sort that must be hidden, as there is between being wounded in a brave battle and being smitten by leprosy.

Often in the hardest and most thankless struggle only God *can* know. This should suffice, but it does not always.

The day has been gray and chill. The very air has seemed to grieve. Was that because " we receive but what we give "?

At dusk Phyllis played and sang, "When the Swallows Homeward Fly," "Rock of Ages," and "Beulah Land." It was like an angel's hand on head and heart.

MARCH 11.

Raining gently all day. The brown cheeks of the hills are washed free of snow at last, and I can hear the full flowing of unfettered streams.

In the soft and sunny air I heard a bluebird's warble, —was it John Burroughs who called that gentle strain " the violet of sound "?

I have been reading Ibsen's " Ghosts." Its unflinching and terrible simplicity and fidelity to truth awes my soul. It has cast a shadow on the hopeful spring air, for I realize that we are all, in some sort, cowards and slaves.

I went down in the lane this morning to fill my toilet pitcher with the soft brook water, — the first time I have stood on the little bridge since before Thanksgiving.

MARCH 14.

At noon we held our breaths to listen to some real bird singing. Toward night we saw three new-comers, picking up their supper in the yard. They had steel-gray heads and dove-gray backs and breasts. To-night the rain is falling with a summer sound; there is faint lightning and distant thunder.

MARCH 14, Evening.

All the days of this month, so far, have been wondrous mild. The birds sing confidently and the old earth shows that she cannot resist cajolery. To-day there has been a good deal of bluster, and one could fancy the wind had kissed a snowbank on its way hither ; but the sun is so bright and the sky so blue that they give an impression of spring warmth everywhere. I walked and loitered and loafed in the woods this afternoon. I saw not one bird, and the wind roared so that I could not have heard one unless he had screamed close by.

The dead leaves were caught up in swirls of air and scattered high and low. The effect was animating, and at a little distance had the appearance of life, as well as motion. By the side of a green-bordered runnel I saw the purple sheen of skunk-cabbage in bloom. The brown water sparkled to its sunlit bottom, and, as it slipped over some roots that reached across its bed, made, at intervals, a gentle gurgle, and then a bubble that

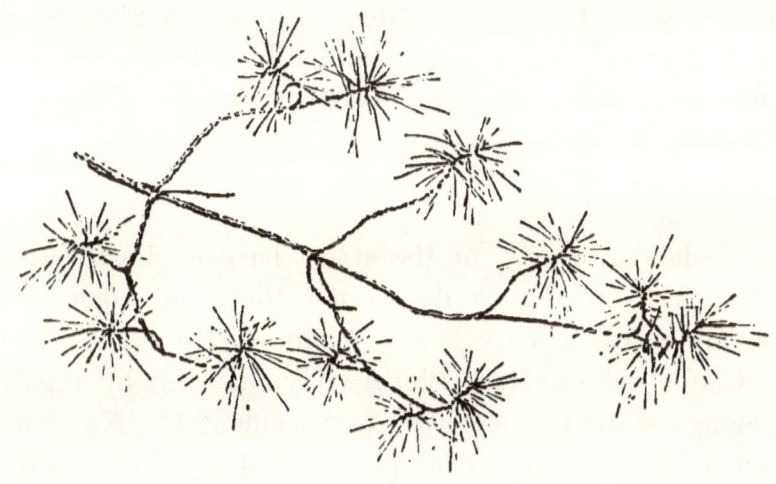

floated down like a crystal island, bearing the glory of sun and tree-top and sky on its shining face.

I went up the slope and crept under the pine-tree whose lowest boughs almost sweep the ground. It was ideal to lie on the fallen brown needles and look up through the branches. The sharp daintiness of the foliage made a wondrous delicate and clear-cut etching on the shining sky, and the voice of the wind was like that of a great harp, muffled, yet longing for full expression.

I ventured on a short ramble in the cedar lot this
afternoon. A keen south wind was there ; the cedars
looked rusty, and great patches of coarse-grained snow
gave the earth a piebald dreariness ; yet the brook in
the alders had a hopeful note ; there was a glimpse of
sky and a half smile of sun, and a distant bluebird pro-
phesied cheerily. To me his song is always " Cheerily !
Cheerily ! "

To-day the spirits of the storm have a ghostly way
of sighing at the windows ; but they play upon our
æolian harps as only storm spirits can.

Could echoes from Pleyel's Hymn, sung by angels
among the stars, sound more transcendental ? No other
music brings such blissful pain. Foolish things to say,
no doubt, about a waxed silken thread and a split stick,
but true.

Pedestrians may now take heart, for the ground is
" settling," and the uneven roads are dry enough to give
a velvety feel to the foot. The streams tinkle and
shimmer in the pale sunshine, and the winter-bleached
and battered world looks comforted.

During my walk I heard a jubilant chorus of robins
and blackbirds. I could not see them, but suspected

from the sound that they were in the wide marsh meadow, where the north winds are broken by the hills and every stray sunbeam gives warmth.

From my chamber window, at sunset, I spied the largest number of robins I ever saw in company. They all paused in their strong flight across the eastern sky and alighted in the tops of the two tall elms in our lane, fine, buxom specimens, full of courageous life. It was a fleeting picture, but after it had vanished something lingered, vaguely sweet, like a dream of wild violets and green-margined streams in sunny places.

The day has been airless and vaguely depressing. As I walked this evening over the dry but excruciatingly uneven roads, croakers and peepers and trillers were in full orchestra, hushing as my steps drew near, only to begin with new vigor when I had passed. By the roadside alder-tassels were shaking out yellow dust, and pussy-willows were showing glistening pearls of buds strung on dark and limber stems.

To-night the winds are asleep and the landscape is lost in a mist. The grass about our south doorstep is getting long and thick, and dock and dandelion have made a courageous stand.

MARCH 21.

Two strange dogs wandered into our yard to-day. They were pitifully lean and hungry-looking.

Phyllis, who takes tender cognizance of all animals,

left her work to feed these two liberally, even cooking mush for them from her scanty supply of "gold-dust" meal, to supplement the cold scraps on hand.

Yesterday it was an abused and half-starved cow that appealed to her sympathies. She gave her potatoes and oats, and told her, in tones eloquent with pity, how she wished she could make her permanently comfortable.

MARCH 23.

The morning after a rainy night was mild and fresh, and full of inspiring odors from the swamps. My early walk was most enjoyable. A flock of wild geese went over in traditional "harrow" style, dropping the wild, soft clamor of their bell-like voices down to me from the exquisite spring blue. I could see the under feathers of the strong-winged leader glisten in the sun.

Before night the weather had changed, and I walked home in a pouring rain, enjoying it as much as if I had been a moss-patch or a jubilant frog. The wet rocks showed beautiful colors, as if the rain had painted them.

MARCH 28.

Up on the pasture lands yesterday the sunlit cedars looked so joyous, with their straight bodies and plumy tops, standing clear against the marvellous blue. To-day they are one with the shadow and sighing born of a wailing wind and darkened sky.

Big rain-drops beat on the panes while we were taking our tea, and now the stars are unveiled and shining. How like the moods of the spirit of man!

MARCH 30.

Yesterday we had rain and sleet, and then a feathery snowfall that lasted several hours. The air was still, and the trees and rocks, being wet, caught and held the downy particles as if by magic. This morning the fantasy had crystallized in the freezing cold, and was slow in dissolving, even in the bright rays of the morning sun. But now, at 2 P.M., the earth is herself again, and smiles all the greener for her temporary masquerade. I have been up on the ledge behind the house. A flock of robin-redbreasts took wing as I approached, and a squirrel scampered off, chattering excitedly. I wished I could make myself invisible, not for their sakes only, but for my own; for I long to see them when they are at home. I found a projection of dry rock for a seat, and a small cedar standing behind me made a desirable spring back, and kept the keen wind from penetrating my hood. The radiant sky, with its dazzling shoals of floating cloud, made me blink; but between the blinks I saw charming things. The sumacs, for instance, on the brow of the ledge, holding garnet velvet clusters in airy relief, with the pale-blue west for background. Down under the apple-tree on the wall I had noticed a quantity of red chaff

scattered among the moss and stones, which proved to
be from sumac bunches. Perhaps this is the work of
squirrels. Do they eat the kernels? Every bit of color
looks intense to-day. I saw three or four raspberry stalks,
beautiful with tints of bloomy grape-purple. It was
pleasant to shut my eyes and listen. A shrub oak at
my left made softest castanets of its crisp leaves in the
brisk wind. Phœbes were calling, with their wonted
gay good humor. If a sunbeam could speak, I fancy its
voice would be like phœbe's.

MARCH 31.

Soft, purplish, hazy skies, and a glamour of sunlight
that looks warm, and would be, but for a strong, south-
east wind that seems to have come from a cold country.
There were northern lights last night. I chanced to be
up and awake at twelve o'clock, and sat by my window
for a time to watch the strange glory. All the heavens
seemed to palpitate as the great waves of color came
and went among the stars.

APRIL.

APRIL 1.

Dreamy sunshine — faintly golden — air like a cheek
of velvet. I have seen a butterfly, sunning himself by
the roadside; a big fellow with glossy-black, cream-bor-
dered wings, and I am sure I heard a real "peeper"
tuning up timidly in the swamp.

The sunlight glitters and looks cheerless. A big crow alighted near the house and stalked about on the ground. The air, the light, and the crow combined called to memory the verse by Lowell;

> " There was never a leaf on bush or tree;
> The bare boughs rattled shudderingly ;
> .   .   .   .
> A single crow on the tree-top bleak
> From his shining feathers shed off the cold sun."

Still very cold and bright. We have had another visit from the crow. I went out afterward to find what he could be after. It was a bone with a trace of marrow left in it. I could see where his strong bill had drilled in search of food.

We hear that there has been a big blizzard. I don't know just where, but its breath is here.

After a rainy night, in my morning walk I heard a mourning dove, and noted the red-brown fringes of the tall elm in the swamp by the roadside. Peepers, quiet in the morning, are vociferous when I return at night.

APRIL 7.

As I came home at twilight in a snow-storm I saw
that the spring grass pricked up daintily through the
light coverlet. The swamp minstrels made real music,
not crowding their notes and deafening the ear as they
often do.

APRIL 8.

Chilly and clouded. The snow is full of moisture,
but is slow in going. The Kenilworth ivy between the
stones in front of our door and the thrifty grass that
keeps it company look wondrous fresh and sparkling in
their snow setting.

Peering among the rubbish in our last year's flower-
plat I found the English violets holding tiny budgets
of purple, and the myrtles nearly ready to blossom.
In the back yard, and around the big rock, there are
conspicuous clusters of celandine, with large, deeply
notched leaves of light green. Clover and daisy roots
are sprouting vigorously.

In the cold sunset I heard a robin singing silver
clear.

The grass is now faintly green in our yard. O, who
does not love this sweet, slow smile of awakening!
East wind bringing mist, peepers piping lustily, and
soft anthems in the moist, gray woods!

After days of chilling wind we have quiet skies and
soft sunlight. I walked a little way in the woods, and

lingered awhile by the brook. It looked so happy with its brown water beaming with warm light, and the old moss-covered tree-roots curved about it caressingly.

I saw just one cowslip in blossom, and plenty of leaf-clusters, and stems rank with promise. Spicebush is bright, with its odd little tufts of odorous yellow.

In a cleft on the south side of a big gray rock I found a cluster of new ferns, very delicate. Some of the fronds were quite unrolled, and looked mature, except for an extreme tenderness of color. They look

related to those in our well. The pine-tree in " its aloofness and its faithful green " was as adorable as ever. I saw stars of glistening thistle-leaves set closely on the earth's breast. In the sun they had a frosty beauty. Gibson calls them " rosettes," and says they take a year to grow.

Clover patches look thrifty, some in shades of blue-green, and others of yellow-green. Blue-flag is shooting up bright green spires in the marsh.

Calamus is not so forward ; and the young aspirants after light are partially sheathed in the remnants of last year's growth, making the beds much more brown than green. Mint is coming in rapidly, with small, dark leaves, purple underside, and succulent purple stems full of aromatic flavor. Balm of Gilead buds are out. From my window they look like oblong rolls of maroon velvet, stuck on nearly at right angles with the upright branches and twigs of the tree.

APRIL 10.

The first thing I saw when I opened the outer door was a dead robin stretched on the turf just beyond the step. His feathers were mussed, but I could see no wound. Perhaps he was struck by a hawk, and falling under the trees could not be secured. One eye was closed, the other partially open and showing the dimness of death. He was cold and stiff, and lay with his innocent throat turned upward to the white morning light. I held him in my two hands tenderly, and wondered, " Where is the living, loving *soul* that sang life's merry song ! "

To-day a large, light hawk swooped down on one of Phyllis' chickens. He tore out a clawful of her pretty white feathers, but was scared off without doing further damage. The air is so cold that even the faintest green in the landscape looks out of place.

APRIL 11, 2 P.M.

It has stormed constantly since early dawn, at first with a moderate wind and snowfall. Now it is like a blizzard. We can see but dimly to the end of our lane, for the mad, blinding whirl. Trees in the more sheltered places, especially apple-trees, are heavily burdened. Not a twig can lighten itself, writhe as it may. Lilac buds are as large as pears in their unseasonable overcoats.

To the windward, however, the snow blows off; our two elms, for instance, toss their tender wreaths of brown, unfettered, though strangely out of place in this incongruous element. The brook flows black, and the silken grass-fringes of the pool are buried deep. What will become of the birds? A sparrow came to our door looking for a bite. A woodpecker here before him drove him away, with a sharp nab at his feathers. The unkindness seemed worse than the wintry air.

How I love a storm! Up in my chamber I opened the south window and knelt before it to feel the wandering flakes on my face and hair, and to come nearer to that " gusty music " swelling in the heavens. It was a fitting hymn to the Almighty, and in it my soul was fain to join exultantly.

APRIL 12.

Very gray and wild. East wind still wailing mightily, and scattering snow. To look out, one could never dream that this is nearly the middle of April. It is growing a trifle warmer, however. The eaves drip little rivers noisily, and great bunches of snow dislodged from the trees are falling continually. I received a good snow-balling on my head and shoulders when I went to the well this morning. A few hours of April sun will work wonders, but we shall be in a world of water.

Great Ring road is blockaded and quite impassable.

APRIL 15.

I have been out raking the dead leaves from our yard. Such ravishing April odors! I am not content to smell them, I wish to eat them. I found an English violet bud. I found the poem too, "A violet," in my memory plat. I thought I had forgotten it. Strange, how things get hidden in the brain and can be dug up, all bright and shining again like buried gold.

APRIL 18.

The apple-tree by my south window now taps softly on the pane, with its queer little fuzzy gray mittens that hold in warm hiding the pink fingers of buds that will be held out in welcome to beautiful May.

Showers in the night, and gentle rain in the morning. The air is warm, and the refreshing drops seem to sparkle with hope and the new life they are helping on. Our English violets appear to have doubled in size and the grass in thickness since yesterday afternoon. Fitful sunshine from a typical April sky, whose tender azure made loving amends for all frowning.

I went up among the cedars and wandered over the rocks and knolls. The delicately austere beauty of leafless twigs and branches was never more apparent.

A clump of huckleberry bushes was indescribably pretty. A dainty tangle of slender drab and gray and coral-tinted stems curving in and out, intertwining with each other, some catching the light sharply, others in deep shadow, and all showing myriads of minute, pointed buds of warm brown.

Phyllis has been digging all the forenoon to get the ground ready for seeds. The swamp maples along the road are decked with fringy tufts of dark crimson. The mourning dove still lingers in our neighborhood with its complaining note. I think it says " O-h, love! love! love!"

APRIL 20.

Morning mild and moist. A gentle, gray mist broods over the land. It is filled with the scent of growing things, and of the wet brown leaves and upturned soil. And there are " a-many birds telling their love in music."

A mist in April or May is always beautiful to the imagination if not to the eye, because it breathes so intensely of hope and new life.

Four blue-jays in the naked thorn-tree near the house this morning. They made it blossom with their heavenly blue.

The little yellow birds' love-notes are as golden-sweet to the ear as their plumage is to the eye.

APRIL 25.

In the gray pallor of earliest dawn I heard a whip-poor-will. I think no other bird has such power to produce melancholy, and in that colorless hush, the piercing, passionate strain seemed the essence of anguish. I felt like covering my ears and crying out:

> " O! bird of love, with song so drear,
> Make not my soul the nest of pain !
> O let the wing that brought thee here
> In pity waft thee back again ! "

APRIL 27.

Apple-tree by south window showing hints of red. Flowering currants putting out blossom-buds, as are the lilacs also.

This day has been lovely with soft, strong wind from the south, a glamour of cloud, pearl and opal tinted, sunlight faint and rosy. The grass is most beautiful in its velvet youngness, and brings out the rocks with artistic tenderness. I have heard a tree-toad: does he prophesy rain ?

I found pink and white wind-flowers on the border of the marsh; drooping among their maroon-tinted leaves, and very pale blue violets. These last are too short-stemmed for nosegays, and in truth looked too celestially fair for earthly hands, as if they had fallen from the

sky and were waiting for translation to their native air.

APRIL. 28.

No rain. A very heavy dew in the early morning that turned to rainbow hues in the sunrise. The weather still warm, with south wind, and tender, pearly sky, clouds soft, but mountainous in shape, with thunder-cap summits. Tree-toad still prophesying. Apple-trees are fast decking themselves with pale-green bunches of leaves. The brook's bed is like a green path through the meadow.

Phœbes are building in the barn-loft. A wren bubbles over happily all day. I have tried to get near enough for a good look at him, but he is so tiny and so nearly the color of the tree bark that I only succeed in making him silent, while he still remains invisible except when on the wing.

Two hours later. — A delicious shower, accompanied by a warm, rushing wind; after that, dead stillness. The evening brought a faint star-shine. Whip-poor-will, grown bold, came near the house and sang piercing clear.

APRIL. 29.

Morning cooler, very fresh and dewy, with pale, hazy sky. Between nine and ten I took a short ramble through the north lot and along the foot of the eastern hill in the pasture. In that sheltered spot the sun fairly burned. I tried to look up at the tree-tops, but could only blink to a state of tearfulness. I broke off a low branch of maple that was thickly set with tiny " knives and forks," as we called them in my childhood.

In the turf of the hillside I saw three openings within a few yards of each other that might be entrances to woodchuck dens. The yellow earth thrown out formed conspicuous mounds, and contained some quite large and heavy stones.

Deep-purple violets studded the short grass, and among them, as if to set off their royal richness, new velvety gray-green leaves of everlasting.

The mosses made an elastic cushion under foot, and the lichened rocks felt alive to the hand. Sweet-ferns are swinging russet-colored tassels from the tips of their russety-brown stems, whose slender length is thickly set with paler russet leaf-buds. In some places the slopes were dotted thickly with an early spring flower whose name I do not know. It has four white toes — five or six sometimes —and looks a little bit like everlasting at first glance. The flower sets close to the ground now, but will soon rise on a stem of several inches. Its odor always suggests "bee-bread." I suspect this flower to be mock everlasting.

Phyllis found a tiny frog in the water-barrel this morning. He looked like the " Pickering," judging from Mr. Gibson's description ; and when put in the brook insisted upon scrambling out and climbing a bulrush.

MAY.

MAY 1.

A real May day, — sunrise rosy ; white birch tops
daintily dim in gauze of palest green; birds in ecstatic
chorus. Apple-tree buds are coral-red; cherry and
peach trees beginning to blossom. Fragrant currant
breathes incense from its clusters of clove-shaped, yellow flowers under my window. I went on a long saunter this morning; found exquisite white violets in the
old orchard meadow between the roads; spied a bough
with a bird's nest on it that I covet to sketch. Phyllis
went with me to the spring of sweet, clear water, where
we drank our fill. The basin of the spring is solid rock;
a little below it, and supplied by the tricklings from
the basin, is a small pool containing a colony of frogs.
They sat around on the edge, or poked their noses above
the water and blinked at us, with an occasional mild
croak that was highly amusing. Primrose-yellow and
pearl-white butterflies fluttering in the roadway. A
woodpecker's peremptory rapping on the top of a tele-
graph pole echoed sharply. I startled a woodchuck
from the corner of the meadow, where he was break-
fasting on dew and young clover, and wondered at the
short-legged creature's speed when I saw him "streak
it " up the hill and disappear in his den under a big rock.
The calamus lot was vivid with shining lances tilting
to the breeze. Raspberry stalks are curving wreaths of
clustered green.

MAY 2.

Another rose-colored morning, incomparably beautiful. I coaxed Phyllis up the road to make a sketch, and
stayed with her until she was ready to come back. She
made two sketches: a bit of swamp with maples, and a
road view, in which I posed with out-spread parasol.

The earth looked so happy, and the heavens so faith-
inviting, it was hard to realize that for at least one-half
the human race life is but a " monster-bearing desert,"
where struggle and tragedy crowd out all gentle loves
and delights.

We heard a bird sing sweetly in minor key, " See!
See! See! Somebody! Somebody! " and another, of a
more blunt and practical turn, took it up in a different
key, and sang, " See-see-see-Blitzy Le-e-elle ! " A
hawk sailed screaming overhead. I never before knew
that his note so closely resembled a blue-jay's.

Tall, woolly stalks of coarse fern stand with fronds
rolled up. Marsh-marigold makes a yellow gleam in
the path of the brook. Half unfolded buds on every
bush catch the light like tiny wings, showing transparent greens and browns and rosy grays; all inimitable
spring's very own.

This afternoon brought a brief shower; big drops
but few, and some mild thunder. Since then the
wind seems to have gone to sleep. The sky remains
clouded. The hush after a shower always makes me
melancholy.

Just now I heard a woodchuck whistle his piercing tremolo, the first I have heard this season.

Crows have been flying low and quite near the house. One was immense, and I saw the blue lustre of his plumage distinctly.

MAY 3.

Very much cooler. This morning I went upon Cedar Hill to call on a favorite tree, — a big, black birch. Its tiny leaves and catkins catching the morning light emphasized the bold strength and beauty of its rough bole and spreading boughs. I found some oval-shaped leaves growing near the ground that appeared to have lived over the winter. They were completely covered on the back with tiny eggs of bright orange color. I broke off a spray of apple-tree and brought it home to sketch.

MAY 4.

Cold south and east wind. Pale sunshine in the morning. At midday I went up among the rocks and tried to find a sheltered place to sit in, but the search-ing air found me out, and I was glad to get in-doors again, although the woods, the rocks, the carpet of warm brown rustling leaves, pricked through here and there with delicate new growth, was pleasant to look on, while the pine and the cedar breathed full sweet to my ear.

Young oaks are tipped with velvety rose-red and pink leaves, that charm the eye all the more for the sober background that still holds its own in the spring woods.

MAY 5.

Much warmer. In the morning a dense mist that stirred and grew thinner at sunrise, and moving, half unveiled, only to veil again the dainty woods, as if loth to expose such tender beauty to the full-orbed day. And they are lingering reluctant still; soft, shadowy shapes against the dream-blue sky, interposing a gentle screen between the earth and sun. As it shifts and wavers, shadows come and go upon the earth, like blushes; and in them one fancies a quickened beating, as of an exquisitively sensitive heart.

The woodland trees are unfolding more and more daily their accordion-plaited leaves; but from my window the trunks and branches are still delicately clear, and cast tremulous shadows on the sunlit brown of the leaf beds that cover the slope. The underbrush is not yet thickened sufficiently to conceal the granite gray of the rocks now freshly painted with a new life of moss.

MAY 6.

Very heavy showers last night and this forenoon. A drying wind has hastened to shake off and absorb all extra wet, and we found it delightful walking after our somewhat late Sunday dinner. Red maples are tasselling beautifully; the young, winged things that are going to be mature seeds one of these days are almost as brightly transparent against the light as colored glass, shading from rich red to golden green. Fern stalks by the roadside stand stiff and straight as soldiers on duty, but with their woolly heads big with dreams of liberty. Tiny, lavender-blue butterflies make one think of violets on the wing. Dandelions dot the short grass thickly, with their glossy yellow discs, between the stone steps and the bridge. Wild columbine swings from stony clefts. I remember what a delight it gave me, when a child, to plunge the leaves of this plant beneath clear water and see them turn to silver there, and then lift them out, as dry apparently as if no water had touched them.

I saw a queer specimen of fungus or toadstool growing in the path to-day. It was precisely like a coarse sponge outwardly, so far as shape and color were concerned, but stiff to the touch, and entirely hollow. When we returned, the dusk was fast closing in. We heard a frog piping from a tall alder bush, and stopped to hunt him up. He was about on a level with our eyes, and allowed us to inspect him quite closely. In the uncertain light, his color appeared to be a rather delicate brown, almost flesh-tint on abdomen and throat.

Last week I thought a pair of robins were going to housekeeping in the thorn-tree opposite my window, and spent a good part of one forenoon watching them.

I had noticed one of the pair, presumably Mrs. Robin, carrying straws, etc., to a snug crotch that will soon be in a bower of sweetest breath. For two or three hours she labored, often flying down to the wet margin of a little pool, and tugging hard at something, that when she rose looked like black earth with fine fibres of root in it. This she deposited in the nest, with much placing, and patting, and smoothing with her breast. Meantime her consort, who lingered indifferently near, made a leisurely toilet, bathing in the brook with many a dip and flirt and flutter, and then sunning himself on a rock, shaking and preening his feathers scrupulously. When he had become quite dry Mrs. Robin went down for a dip while he came near the nest as if to see that no harm befell it. The little housewife performed her ablutions in much quicker time, however, as became a woman of business, and very soon resumed work. How direct and full of meaning is her every motion! She seems to know just what she needs, and just how and where to get it. A woodpecker came and tapped on the body of the tree, but was given to understand that it was no time for receptions. A chipmunk ventured near, but scampered off again. He will doubtless have an eye and a tooth, if he can, on the young birds when they arrive.

I am pleased to anticipate having such interesting neighbors.

I can hear a chickadee calling in the peculiarly

mournful minor key that he sometimes affects. It always sounds incongruous with his cheery "*personnel.*" One could fancy his little love were dead and gone, and he was trying to say, "We two together no more."

MAY 8.

Yesterday was a perfect day. Glorious skies of sunny blue, apple-blossoms odorous and pink, bumble-bees and honey-bees humming a dreamy bass that made a delight-

ful undertone for the winds singing among the new leaves. After sunset I went out into the open meadow, and, leaning on the big rock, faced the great sky. The west was transparently golden where the horizon line of tree fringes touched. The new moon was a thread of silver. No words could speak the deep sense of beauty, and peace, and grateful joy with which my soul ran over.

This morning dawned crisp and clear. The clouds have come in caravans since, all dark-colored on the under side and bringing wind, as they always do. I heard the note of an oriole — the first — piercing sweet and clear above all the bird-medley this morning.

I have seen nothing of my two robins lately, and am

afraid they have deserted their nest. I cannot think why. Every cloud has blown itself beyond vision. The noon sun was fervid, but there was the freshest of breezes. The world is as brilliant as a spring world can be. There are myriads of maples tossing their winged seed-clusters of silvery green, pale terra-cotta, and vivid crimson, transparent and shining against the perfect azure of the sky.

The meadow where I walked is overrun with violets and dandelions. Spreading boughs of dogwood blossoms gleam white against a clump of cedar on the woody hill. White-birch leaves shine in the sun like fluttering bits of glistening satin. The tops of oak-trees are terra-cotta red, delicately conspicuous among the tender shades of green around them.

Down in the spring water-cresses are in blossom ; fine white flowers that at first glance suggest sweet alyssum. The stems are several inches above the water. Red sorrel is painting the meadow slopes in long streaks of soft color.

Strawberry-vines are thick with buds and blossoms. After sunset I sat on a flat rock out in the open to watch the flight of a night-hawk. I could see the white bars on the underside of his wings. Such soaring, such spasmodic flapping, such zigzagging and diving ! I marvelled that he could keep it up so long without alighting. I wonder how he makes the hollow sound with which he descends. After he had disappeared

around the hill I went into the edge of the wood to try
if I could see my favorite bird whose siren singing
made the green aisles ring. I failed; but it was happi-
ness to be there with the pure gold of the sky looking
in through the pencilled tree-tops.

MAY 10.

A week ago to-day an azalea in bud (a potted plant
from the hot-house) came to me, filling my room with
something that seems like the presence of the pure in
heart. I put it on my narrow window-sill, and grieved
a little that it should have been taken from its native
surroundings. But its old lover, the sun, came and
kissed it, and the tender skies smiled down upon it in its
exiled life. The south wind wooed it, and now it has
eight snow-pure blossoms, all rejoicing together. I dimly
feel the lesson.

MAY 11.

Very cool; south-east wind. Went after some dogwood blooms that have been beckoning me of late.
Made a sketch of a small spray. Rain began a little
after noon. The bees are still hard at work in the
apple-blossoms.

How exuberantly the birds sing on such a day! My
favorite alone, whose name and plumage I know not,
has power to enchant the air; and there are many others
not so musical, but very bright and sociable. "Drink

your teas," "whichers," and one that says over and over
with saucy abruptness, " Quit that ! quit that !"

The wrens have once more left the porch. Year after
year they used to build there, but one unlucky spring a
pair of phœbes got in before them, all settled, with a

nest full of eggs. The wrens began a pitched battle,
and one day when the male bird was out of sight Mrs.
Phœbe was killed. When he returned he appeared
overcome with grief at his loss, and distracted with
anxiety concerning the eggs. He hovered over the nest
crying and calling helplessly, and finally carried them
all away, each one separately, by piercing it with his
bill. The poor little wife was picked up from the grass

where she had fallen, and buried out of his sight. But he came back persistently and lingered in the lilac close by, and mourned disconsolately.

The wrens were left conquerors of the field; but for some reason they were not comfortable, and finally left for good. And although regularly every season since, a pair have come and commenced to build, they have invariably left in a few days.

Last week I was quite sure that at last we were to have tenants; the little builder seemed so ambitious, and her consort so overrunning with hopeful song, as if tragedies were unheard-of in the sweet, spring world. But they are gone for sure, after all. Can it be a case of ghost, or traditional conscience? The porch is evidently haunted.

EVENING.

The rain lasted but an hour or so. Mists are rising ghostly with moonlight.

After I had put out my bedroom lamp, I pulled up the window-shade for a good-night look, and was bewildered to see, spanning the wet meadow through which our brook winds, a most exquisite arch. Perhaps it would not be correct to call a mystical creation of moonlight and fog a rainbow, as it was without iridescence. It was a perfect bow nevertheless, and so weird and unlooked-for that I stood spellbound a moment, and then awakened Phyllis to help me look and wonder.

Both ends of the arch appeared to rest in the bed of the

stream ; and where the broad, pearly band crossed the eastern sky, it made a faintly luminous track, so transparent that we could see the stars look through it; for

the mists were not so heavy as to quite obscure the sky. The moon, which is in its first quarter, was low in the west.

It was a spectral picture, with the apple-blossoms breathing " odors pure and white " and the deep stillness broken only by the whip-poor-will. It was like Hope's phantom.

MAY 12.

In the cedar lot this morning I heard a bird say very distinctly and in the pertest fashion, "Wait till you get it!" A cat-bird was in a tangle of melody on a white birch near the brook. He spied me directly, and his song soon ceased, to be replaced by a snarl of dissatisfaction. Heard a field cricket — the first; note timid and uncertain, but welcome as a happy thought to me, for I do love their " speech among the grasses."

> " Many and many a year hereafter
>   You will hear the same blithe tune :
> For though you should outlive laughter,
>   . Crickets still will chirp in June."

Crows were in a great state of noise and commotion,

changing their position every instant. I found it burning
hot in the sunshine, but pleasantly cool under the cedars,
where many a cushioned rock offered an inviting seat.
A heavenly wind breathed through the dark-plumed
tops, and a thousand silvery notes floated to my ear.

Maples, butternuts, chestnuts, and birches are gen-
erously leafy; walnuts and oaks are more cautiously
economical.

Even now the latter still hold some of their old
leaves. The new ones are so beautiful in shape and
coloring. I wish they might be always young.

The woods are flushed with their velvety pinks and
the warm reds of the winged maples. The western
sky was daintily blue, the distant tree-tops golden-green
against it. Wild honeysuckle is thickly budded.

Huckleberry-bushes are reddish-brown with cluster-
ing, bell-shaped buds and blossoms. Yellow cinquefoil,
with its pretty five-fingered vine, covers the ground in
large beds, trailing a "light of laughing flowers"
among the dark club-mosses. Knots of blue violets
lie on the meadow's breast. Some of the grasses are
beginning to flower. Apple-blossoms, faintly rosy and
sensitive to every puff of air, are faltering down to rest
lightly on the crisp grass. The foot-paths even are
paved with their silken daintiness.

Only the second week in May, and their glory almost
over!

At home in the apple-tree, a little bird with brilliant

buttercup-yellow throat and breast. He wore a neck-
lace of jet black, with long black lines diverging from
it over the chest. His back held a few white feathers,
but I am not sure about the rest. They seemed to be
black and light gray. He was very busy picking among
the apple-blossoms, and had a low but ear-piercing cry,
like a small hinge shrieking for oil.

MAY 13.

The earth, the air, the sky! They might all be
Eden's own. I have taken no walk; everything worth
seeing seemed to come. — birds, bees, and butterflies,
while showers of apple-blossoms freighted the south
wind. The long morning was dewy and cool. An
oriole with orange-yellow and black coat haunted the
tall elm, and chanted, bugle-clear, "Wait a little, jewel,
jewel; I'll be there! I'll be there!"

The lilacs are in full and perfect bloom, and attract
many varieties of butterfly. I have seen a very large
yellow one, black-bordered and black-streaked; a medi-
um-sized velvety dark one, that looked like the earlier
spring butterflies; and the common little primrose-yel-
lows, that have such a pretty way of floating in pairs.
The gnats are on hand too, and now toward night the
mosquitoes have come to give the soul a lesson in patience. The night-hawk was out again about noon to-
day, careering madly through the sun-bright heavens.

I suppose he was fishing in that scintillant sea of air for his dinner.

Cricket voices are fast multiplying.

EVENING.

Glorious, full-toned, odorous — pale silvery light, and buoyant movement of shadows. Saw the first firefly light his tiny lamp under the shade of an apple-bough, as if, like a thrifty housewife, he could not afford to have a breath of air puff it out.

MAY 15.

A cold north-west wind, that the bright sun fails to warm. During my short stroll in the meadow I saw one wild geranium (crane's-bill) flower. Wild columbine in large families among the rocks caught the light on their rich red and yellow horns. There was just one cluster of wild fennel in flower. In a sheltered hollow grew some early daisies, the lavender-tinted kind, with fine soft petals and hairy stems. I brought home a young budded spray of tulip-tree (white-wood). Its transparent, pale leaves, the stems, the buds, all looked like wax, and are of the most perfectly pure green that I ever saw anywhere, except on the back, wings, and legs of a certain green grasshopper.

In the afternoon took the cart-path woodward and visited the brook. Jack-in-the-pulpit was there, growing nearly two feet in height, with stalk as large as my little

finger. On the way I saw blackberry and raspberry
vines in bud. Grapevine leaves are downy soft and
crimson edged,— little fans
set round to screen the
blossom-clusters from too
much sun or wind.

MAY 16.

Red sunrise. N o t a
drop of dew on the grass
this morning. A g o o d
time for an early tramp,
but I did not get into the
woods until between nine
and ten. The b r e e z e s
were soft, under a sky of
pale azure, but it was
warm walking over the ups and downs of the way, and
I was sorry to have a wrap with me. I walked so far,
and was so tired, that even a crooked stick was wel-
comed to lean upon. The undergrowth is brightened
by clumps of wild azalea. I saw in an exposed clearing
where a frost had killed tall ferns that were just ventur-
ing to uncoil, and the young leaves of oak saplings
which were already taking on new growth.

A *whicher* bird called with monotonous persistence,
but I could not find him. When I sat down to rest by

the cart-path, it was on a fallen and decayed tree-trunk.
A large-winged bird flew up with a whirr. At my feet
the ground was moist. Mossy rocks were huddled
together, and among them grew white violets. The
shyest and tenderest little faces they have, out of all the
world of flowers. In wet weather this path is probably
overflowed.

A pair of birds with plumage of écru and tan color
were frolicking together among the leaves. But my
eyes were holden to-day rather more than usual, I fancied;
and when I had gotten back, I wondered if it were not
true that " home-keeping hearts are happiest," after all.
It looked so pleasant near the lonely house. I could
see the distant hills wrapped in a lavender haze, and I
fancied the great clumps of lilac flowers lent their color
to the air, while giving of their sweets to humming-bird
and butterfly and bee. Another parable from nature.
During my walk I secured a fine branch of maple
" wings, " as richly colored as any autumn spray. It
is lovely now, in a vase of clear glass, and leans across a
water-color picture of Phyllis', contrasting with its wide
blue sky as if it were again on its native heath.

MAY 17.

Sun a distinctly outlined, fiery ball at rising; its light
like a clear stain of flame-color on everything it touched.
Before night the sky was thick with clouds, sombre
blue-gray in the south. Strong south-east winds bearing

a faint mist. I found some very large buttercups by
the roadside, and thought aloud,

> " How golden the buttercup blooms by the way,
> A song of the joyous ground! "

MAY 18.

Clear again and no rain yet. The grass on the steep
slope of our yard is turning tawny. Its roots find little
nourishment on account of the rock-bed underneath, and
feel the drought keenly. The little garden by the rock
will suffer if refreshment does not come soon; while as
for our well, — but we will not borrow trouble if we can
help it. Such debts demand a high rate of interest.
There is a sort of fascination for me in very dry weather.

MAY 19.

A thunder-shower at nine o'clock last night, followed
by more showers at intervals ever since. Inexpressibly
welcome and reviving. The clouds are dense, and bring
waves of darkness that make twilight in the house.
How everything rejoices, growing visibly! The birds
have been in ecstasies. My gay oriole has made himself
especially " numerous, " glancing here and there and
everywhere all day, with a note as intense and striking
as his own plumage. I saw an indigo bird for a moment
this morning, on a rock under the apple-tree. In a
moment he was off, flying low over the wet meadow.

The bark of the apple-trees is soaked to sepia-brown, dappled with lighter shades of the same rich color, and the gray lichen growing upon it is tinted with verdigris-green. The great clusters of lilac flowers, bowed over with the weight of a myriad rain-filled chalices, look silvery cool. As I pass them on my way through the yard, I cannot resist treating my face to a plunge bath, with many a loving sniff in their odorous freshness.

Such jubilee of birds in the golden dawn, heralding golden days!

We were surprised this morning by the arrival of a mutual friend, who spent the day with us. We all sat out of doors, under the pink and white apple-trees, and he read to us from " The Light of the World. " In the evening we walked to the old home and sat with some friends before a merry fire. But it was very lonely. Through all the light chat and laughter our hearts were listening — as if the missing voices must come back, to mingle with our own, as of old. The hazy sky looks hot. The faint light from the new moon, the great clouds of blossoms hanging in the trees, made our return walk a delight; for despite all woes foregone or to come, the soul must respond to this caressing beauty.

MAY 20.

Still dark with fierce scuds of rain. We pull our curtains up and away from the windows, that the wild joy of tossing tree-top and swift clouds drifting may seem to come nearer. A glorious storm, that makes one covet a league-long tramp in divided skirts and top boots.

The rain ceased last evening, but the north-east gale is scarcely abated, and brings a chill that Hosea Biglow would say is much more like a mayn't than May! The sunless sky still looks a watery waste. Many leaves are tattered; now and then a cluster torn off lies on the ground. The fruit-stems of apple-trees have been shaken down by thousands. But the grass has fairly leaped in its growing, and the woods have clothed themselves as by a miracle since the rain began. Already we are near the perfection of June foliage.

I hear no birds, except an unquenchable *whicher*, and a robin whose high and dauntless call, like that of a blue-jay, seems a vital part of all wild weather. At ten o'clock, when I went for a wood saunter, the rank grass was beaded with wet. The long, winding path is full of tender growths, so tender that I shrank from setting a rude heel among them. Every variety of fern seems to have made its *début*,

from the tall ones whose tops appear to float, to the
low-clustered, lace-patterned kind that weave their
cloudy draperies near the ground. Wild honeysuckle

made immense bouquets,
growing in large clumps
of glowing rose-color and
palest pink. Mock honey-
suckles grew near, and
every few steps I came
upon their slender, sway-
ing stems, drooping pale-
green udders of emptiness.
Sometimes they are covered
with a soft bloom of creamy
pink t h a t outrivals the
choicest fruit; e v e n a s
pretty airs and graces by
their winsome brightness do
sometimes eclipse sterling worth.

The gray-headed dandelions, now so plentiful everywhere, showed many disfigurements, — silvery locks,
all matted in meek token of the storm's harsh ways.
Some of them were quite bald, and looked as if they
needed caps to match the somewhat elaborate, though
crumpled, ruffs they wore.

I found three lavender daisies that were pink. These
flowers, like the wild geraniums, seem to run the gamut
of shades between blue and pink; but the pink is

always a surprise. The woods seemed filled with a sombre spirit to-day, born perhaps of dimness and damp, and the cold, sighing wind that keeps the trees restless under a sunless sky. Suddenly I came upon an opening near the path where at one time some wood-choppers had pitched their tent. Most of the timbers had been removed, but the earth floor was still thickly carpeted with straw, and large, black shreds of tarred paper were lying about. Two pairs of shoes grotesquely posed gave human interest to the picture, while an empty tomato-can, and a spice-box with lid rusted on, hinted at fireside comforts. Those woodmen belonged to a reckless set. We used to hear them, on quiet nights, carousing drunkenly. Had the sober woods and the pure night skies no message for them? Did remorseful memories and good resolutions awake with the dawn, only to be drowned in fresh libations? But the old shoes were like dead men, and told no tales.

MAY 27.

Up to this date, moon's change to last quarter, rain, fog, mist, almost continually. Just before these wet days we observed a peculiar condition of the barometer: a spiral twist, somewhat like an auger in the centre, extending the whole length of the tube.

The sun to-day has shone hot and bright, but the wind is still from the south, and blows strong. Dog-day skies.

I have been down to the white-wood tree. The protecting bud-sheaths, which in my ignorance I mistook for the buds themselves, have burst and disclosed the real bud much darker green. The sound of the broad, cool leaves as they fluttered together was precisely like the pattering of raindrops.

From my hammock to-day I saw my old friend, the woodchuck, who has had his domicile in the corner of our yard for years. He looks very gray, but is quite agile, and appears to enjoy the young clover fully as much as ever.

MAY 28.

More heavy fog in the morning, clear sunshine at midday, followed soon by rainy-looking clouds drifting up from the south. The air is quite cool. Some of the clouds have looked cold and hard, like waves whipped by the wind. Afterward they took on a tattered appearance, as if they had been violently torn apart. The wind has had a hissing sound, as if a cyclone were in progress. It makes me think of water around a steamship keel. A few big drops have set the leaves a-quiver.

EVENING.

A thunder-shower. Inky blackness.

MAY 29.

At last a north-west wind, cool, clear, and dazzling bright. From my window the green earth looks as if fresh created. Shadows weave their fantastic patterns on the wind-rippled meadow. The brook glitters like molten silver, while among the waving fern-plumes that haunt its path the calamus lances bend and shine.

Above the sonorous chanting of the wind I can hear just one bird singing. The song is not elaborate, but full of a placid cheerfulness that seems the very soul of this pure and sun-sweet air. The storm, we hear, has worked terrible havoc from Minnesota to Kentucky,— floods, cyclones, snow, etc. The echo of it has reached even to our sheltered Nunnery.

MAY 30.

A remarkably weird sunset. It made me think of Browning's

" Roland to the dark tower came."

As I was walking home it was impossible to avoid turning and looking at it many times.

This wondrous May weather cannot prevent a deep unrest.—perhaps because I have not had my usual supply of work. Even the buttonhole man, with his little black hearse full of fine work, and his insultingly paltry payments, no longer comes this way. Spring cleaning at the Nunnery is over. I put the last touches to my room yesterday. It looks so snug and home-y to me, while from my windows the green world, thrilling with the joy of life, makes me long to be in perfect

accord with it.   " For the effort of the soul, like that of
nature, is ever to return to its repose."

Just now there appears to be an ocean of leisure to

swim in.   Why can I not dive in it and bring up one
tiniest pearl, or at least find a shell on the shore and
repeat intelligibly the song it sings?

I have heard that " it is better to be, than to deline-
ate being," but I know that life is never satisfactory
without some sort of doing.

A friend has sent me " Lorna Doone." I am reading it as slowly as possible, actually making delays, so as to keep it a growing life in my present. For the characters, and everything concerning them, will be alive and warm so long as I do not reach *finis*. When I have done that they will begin to turn faint and cold, and drift towards that "long burial aisle of the past," whither countless other ghosts have preceded them.

JUNE.

JUNE 5.

Rain every day. Unprecedented "spell of weather" truly! Is it going to "rain forty-one days and break the record"? We have had the open windows of heaven dripping upon us for three weeks already. This afternoon the sun has glimmered faintly, but to-night the west is shrouded in solid clouds of leaden blue. As I sat in my hammock under the apple-tree, at sunset, I heard a cuckoo, and saw a bird rise in the air, singing as he soared. He remained but a few seconds, then fluttered down again still singing, and was lost among the tree-tops. It was a blithe song and a pretty sight.

Our woodchuck neighbor has been out for an airing. Phyllis' hens all gathered around him as he lay reclined before the entrance of his den. They craned their curious necks, and peered and cackled and commented hysterically as they inspected him; but he was apparently as indifferent to their interest as the rock

under him.   By this time there should be a hen-tradi-
tion of the gray woodchuck and his affairs ; but a hen
has apparently no memory, and draws no conclusions.

Ox-eyed daisies are blossoming, gleaming white in a
mist of purple-gray grasses and Dutch clover.

JUNE 7.

This same sweet seventh of June is my birthday.   It
is Phyllis' also, with precisely two years in her favor ;
so we have been standing together before her biggest
looking-glass and paying each other the most stupen-
dous compliments, by way of mutual encouragement !
Phyllis declares the glass has gotten gray and wrinkled,
and that she must hasten to buy a new one !   And I
laughed and made merry, wand as secretly heavy-
hearted in the presence of Old Time, — like the king's
jester who prayed so pathetically, " Lord, be merciful to
me, a fool."

There are times, I believe, in every life, when all the
past appears like a farce over which the gods might weep.

To-night when I came to my room I found pinned to
a corner of my glass these lines :

> I am content,
> For upon my heart
> Age can never creep;
> And when at last in stillest night
> I seem to sleep,
> A birthday comes to me in truth,
> The gift it brings, *immortal youth*."

This morning I went out to meet the sure welcome of the fields. The sun-steeped grasses were breathing incense after the showers of last night, and all the leaves and stems were full of fragrance.

Ferns leaned out from the gray wall's shelter, in happy family groups, bowing and beckoning all together, as if they would say, " Come and be one of us; here are cushioned rock, and lichen-painted tree, and last year's wind-heaped leaves. Sit and lean and be gay with a holy gayety, and let your careful and troubled thoughts go dancing with the shadows rejoicing in the wind and sun ! "

A butterfly, all lilac and silver, spread buoyant wings and hovered along the way alluringly. Eye-bright blossoms in the friendly grass shone blue and pure as the glances of little children ; venerable dandelions, stiff and tall, were shaking hoary heads at their gay young sisters as if they had forgotten their own coquettish youth. I saw daisy-buds tightly folded, hearts of gold swelling within ; buttercups glistening, and scattering their riches like prodigals. I heard the south wind in the trees like the sound of soft wings beating. A cat-bird's roundelay came brokenly from a corner of the field, where, doubtless, he was singing to his mate, patient on her nest of hope. High in the dazzling upper air a chimney-swallow skimmed and circled, twittering rapturously. I thought I could imagine the contrast he must feel between that boundless purity and freedom and the foul darkness of his narrow home. I thought it would be like the grave again, after resurrection, and wondered how he could ever go back.

JUNE 11.

This morning I was awakened by the clear carolling of a robin not far from my chamber window. The lusty notes had routed my dreams, and all my daylight thoughts came rallying to that "Cheer! Cheer! Come here, come here! My dear, come here! here! here!" even as soldiers, roused from sleep, respond to the *reveille*.

But, physically, I was sluggish, and the sweet, gray dawn was good to rest in, so it was full seven o'clock when I went out for my short walk, and I had missed the most desirable part of the day; for the wide east was now blazing with the unclouded sun and the zenith blue was pale and thin. Gad-flies, fierce for blood, followed me like so many cannibals. But the green-bordered road was still cool : its undisturbed dust dew-darkened and velvet-soft with shadows ; a narrow, rambling way, full of leisurely curves, with a mid-wreath of may-weed and grasses to testify that it is not of the world worldly, but a path of peace.

A dream day. Sun a flame-colored sphere in a tawny haze. All shades of green are intensified by a sort of ruddiness in the light. The hills are blue with a smoky vapor. Scarcely a leaf stirs. The air rings with bird-notes. At this moment I hear a robin's song. It sounds just as the singer moves and works, — clearheaded.

The crows and blue-jays have been holding a grand pow-wow over High Rock. On cool, quiet, dim days like this, I think the birds do not retire to the woods at all, not even for a *siesta*.

The air, the trees, the meadow, all are alive with glancing wings. From my window I saw a wren assail a cat-bird, diving down with most unamiable note. The latter did not retaliate, but got out of the way in a contemptuously leisurely fashion.

In the edge of the woods my wonderful singer is pouring out his song. I think he is a thrush, but cannot see him, and if I could should not know the difference between a "hermit" and a "wood." One bird says, "See the pretty creature!" Another, "Sweet as peaches, sweet as peaches," over and over with bewildering rapidity. I like them all better than that tiresome oven-bird with his piercingly persistent exhortation, like a Primitive Methodist, to go "To church! to church! to church! to church!"

The leaves of the apple-trees are bitten and crumpled, much to their disfigurement. I found a gray worm rolled up in one leaf on the bough by my window. Some of the leaves are covered with a purple-gray deposit that may be eggs, or some sluggish parasite. I cannot see them distinctly. Big black ants are running continually on the body and branches of the tree. The little black hornets are flying about my chamber, looking for holes in which to deposit germs for another generation, with provender to sustain them until they are able to make their entrance into a world of action and shift for themselves.

Sometimes a spool from my work-basket is chosen, — one from which the end labels have been removed. Tiny green worms are imprisoned, and the opening plugged with clay and left to time and nature.

I saw the daintiest of winged things to-day, out under the apple-tree, of palest azure and white down; a moth of some sort, I suppose, but it was shaped more like a bird, and might have been a winged carrier from fairy-land. I slipped my hand under it as it floated near me, and it lingered on my palm long enough to make me wish for a microscope.

The wrens are very quarrelsome to-day. I saw them just now threatening a robin. Heavy thunder-showers at dusk, with fierce, forked lightning east and south of us. Delicious scents from the drenched earth and flowers. Fireflies joyously brilliant. Air cooler.

June 16.

Very hot. Field daisies (ox-eyed) in their glory. Humming-birds among the weigelas by our window; chestnut-trees wearing plumes, still green and closely braided.

June 17.

Excessively hot. Lavender skies. Orange-colored sun and moon. Wondrous medley of birds mornings and evenings. That nameless singer came near the house at dawn, and pricked holes in my morning nap with "cimeters of sweetness." I dreamed I was in the woods, and the bird's song as it floated on the air became visible in the form of filmy lace that rested airily on the branches of the trees. Here and there the pattern was intensified and seemed to symbolize the more emphatic notes of the song. It was woven music. The evening is most beautiful, with fireflies and moonlight and the cool breath of dew. Dim skies and few stars. Whip-poor-wills' impassioned strain beating the passive air.

June 18.

Very hot in the morning; torrid sun and hazy sky and blue distances. Cooler in the evening; wind strong from the south.

We hear of seventeen-year locusts ravaging the country, which seems to bode ill for our State.

Heavy fog after a close night. Hedges beautiful, a riot of wild vines and a ravishing odor from grape blossoms. Elder-trees are in thick bud. I fancy the

daisies never were so large and pure-looking. Oceans of buttercups; a meadow near our out-of-sight-and-sound neighbor is a sea of gray-topped grasses flecked with yellow. Hop-clovers lean and spread themselves in the road border; or is it something else? The leaves and stalk resemble sweet clover, but the blossom, although hop-shaped, is yellow. Saw one or two tall, branching stems of small lilac flowers like asters. Blackberry blossoms in cloudy wreaths by the wayside. Cherries prematurely dropped, bright as coral, on the trodden earth of the street. Blue-flag in blossom, tall and cool in the "dark light" of shaded water-courses.

AFTERNOON.

Mild south wind, thunderous and showery. Faint star-shine at evening, lightning, fireflies; an exquisite night.

June 20.

Morning soft and breezy; skies beautiful with great shimmering gray clouds. The woods and blossoming fields are tenderest gray in the half-veiled light. Afternoon skies June-blue, with clearly defined clouds of dazzling white. In the brilliant light I walked down to see my white-wood tree, only to find its tulip flowers over-blossomed, many of them decayed and falling. Saw a clump of faintest pink wild roses growing low in the meadow grass.

Evening.

A sudden and heavy shower. There is no wind, and the rain falls with a dreamy quietness. Now and then a flash of golden lightning makes a vivid *silhouette* of the apple-tree against the southern sky. The air has been heavenly all the afternoon. I sat in the hammock full two hours before the rain, enjoying the cool, clouded sky and the vespers of the birds. My peerless one sang divinely clear. As it grew later the dusk blossomed into a perfect carnival of fireflies, whose fitful light imparted an indescribably spiritual effect to the already sweet pallor of the daisied fields. In all my life I have never felt nearer nature's deep heart than I do to-night, and I thank God that it is so.

June 23.

Still torrid, although the sky looks September-cool. Phyllis brought me a great armful of crimson roses, the

old-fashioned, almost single ones that always bring me
memories of grass pinks, sweet-williams, and a host of
other flowers that my sainted mother loved.

JUNE 24.

Very hot at sunrise, but growing breezy and cooler,
until at four o'clock there was a very perceptible chill.

The sky, heavily clouded, gave
down a few sprinkles of rain. Now,
at six, there is every indication of an
easterly storm. The meadows, ripe
for the scythe, are so beautiful,
clothed in misty purple and set
with daisy stars. Baby birds just
out of the nest utter quavering
notes.

> " Stillness accompanied with sounds so soft
> Charms more than silence."

The surplus apple-tree leaves, mottled with brown
and yellow, and prematurely fallen, make a royal
carpet on the dark earth, between our back door and
the wood-house. Numberless times every day they
attract my eye, and fill me with a deep though unde-
finable delight.

> " If any ask me Why?
> 'Twere easier to die
> Than tell ! "

From my window I can see the daisies look up clearly, with their "golden eyes bright as hope," and as brave and hardy.

Blue-flag is blooming down in the hollow, with its root in the brown brook. Calamus and mint are there too, rank and odorous; and over them butterflies dip and hover the whole day long.

At night the marsh is alive with fireflies. They love a moonless, black night, and a warm air, thick with damp, for their revels.

I never saw them more brilliant than they were last evening, as I sat in my unlighted room, watching. I had a little five-year-old girl in my lap, who was watching too. I had been telling her that they had wings and legs, and looked, in the daytime, very much like other bugs. "But," she said, "*these* take *lanterns* with them when they go up in the sky."

All night a strong south wind went rushing through the woods, — it was a river of peace to the ear, — and the crickets sent up their sweet tunes trustfully. When I laid my head on my pillow I felt as if I were being rocked in Nature's cradle, to her most motherly lullaby.

JULY.

JULY 16.

Home again, after nearly two weeks' absence! Everything here, from the wreaths of green on our tossing elms to the humble plantain

at our feet, beams with welcome. Dandy Jim looks at us with eloquent eyes and follows Phyllis about, as if he never wished to lose sight of her again. He had his own cosy gray chamber, with its scarlet-curtained window and white bed, which he could keep or leave at will; and he could not have suffered from hunger or thirst in such friendly weather, but it is plain enough that he has not relished keeping bachelor's hall. We three have celebrated our home-coming by living out of doors all this day, among the green-gold shadows of our own roof-tree. Phyllis has sketched, and I have swung in the hammock, below the robins' nest, and read aloud.

At noon we spread a big napkin on the sweet grass, and with new-laid eggs boiled to solid white and gold, milk, bread and cherries, we dined sumptuously, and, like the gods, wanted nothing.

I am grieved to find that nearly all my delicate seeds have perished in the ground. No candytuft, no pansies, no alyssum, nothing that I love but mignonette. It seems dreadful to have "moon shets" and "tossel flowers" flaunting their colors above the dead germs of my darlings. But such is life!

Since the sun went down I have been for a stroll, on a favorite road, lingering gratefully until long past twilight. When I pined in the noise and glare of the city, how I craved to be alone, once more, in the dewy dusk, on that same piece of memory-hallowed earth! Nowhere else can the solemn stars so smile for me, nor the stately trees so lean to me. There is a sympathetic, consoling presence in every fence corner and under every leaf and bush.

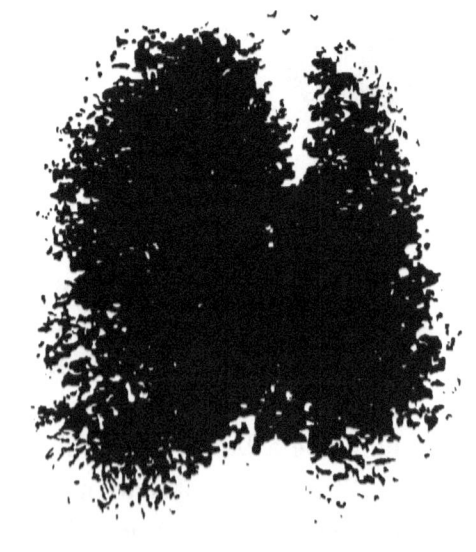

The glow-worms' still lamp in the darkness, the rustle of a wind-waved bough at my side, the wild cry of some restless night-bird, all come home to me, as if " its soul had been a part of mine, and claimed it back once more." There I can breathe my most daring wish, and confess my bitterest folly and defeat, fearless and unashamed. I can smile, I can weep, I can sing, I can shout; I know I shall meet with no selfishness, no coldness, no critical nor curious eyes. The Indulgent Invisible that reigns in that kingdom will still reach me the hand of good-fellowship !

JULY 17.

The purple clover, silvered with mist, is most beautiful; so is the gently rising knoll, with its low brow haloed by the pale glory of blossoming grass. The dark woods lie just beyond and overflow with song. A morning-glory, white with little dabs of blue, has unfolded to-day. In our dearth of garden flowers and other happenings we regard this as an event!

JULY 27.

Very cool and fresh. The air is like September. Every sight and sound teems with memories — memories that are like " tears from the depths of some divine despair."

AUGUST.

AUGUST 7.

An exquisite day. The dawn was wreathed with gold-touched mists. The softest of shadows are moving now; the warm-scented air a full tide of restful sounds. How the soul longs for the peace and harmony it *feels* in nature!

"*Drink your tea*" birds have been singing all the afternoon. Towards evening a heavy shower; afterwards a dead calm, misty and melancholy.

AUGUST 8.

Fresh and breezy, cool hazy sky. "Northern lights" last eve, at bedtime. I foolishly lingered, undressed, by the open window to enjoy the heavenly light and air, and was, in consequence, chilled and sleepless all night.

After sewing awhile this morning, my stitches all ran together, so I dropped my work and ran out for an airing, and to see how the huckleberries were doing on Cedar Hill. Filled my pail and returned by half-past eleven; tired in one sense, but rested in another. I brought home some bunches of sweet-fern, shaded richly with red and brown. Every thistle bloom held, on its lavender cushion, a butterfly. "The cedars spake with deep content." The great, cool sky was full of cloud islands, where winds and sunbeams lived lovingly together.

AUGUST 9.

A real summer day. I took a short walk, after breakfast, up the shady road, toward the old house.

How divinely *new* the air was! Emerson says, " Ah, you do not know what is in the air !"

I pulled some wreaths of wild clematis (travellers' joy) from the dewy riot of the hedge, a cat-bird in a maple near scolding continuously in very feline tones, meanwhile, though I tried to assure her I meant no harm.

Of late a tree-toad has come to live in the apple-tree close to my window, and every day, at odd intervals, he gives vent to a few startling notes. This afternoon I heard a timid answer from another toad, in another tree. Does this point to a toad romance?

Out from the shadows, at the foot of a tall shrub, leans a spray of buttercups. The sunlight falls on its sheen of yellow flowers, and brings them into bold relief. Were I a painter, I would put that bit of glory on canvas.

How the locusts chant, and chant! The swamp is now bedecked with " sober herbs," in fullest blossoming. Pink spires of hard-hack, and spreading, gray-white tufts of boneset, and a profusion of reddish-purple blooms, whose name I ought to know, but do not. Even the alder bushes are not without charm; they have such cool-looking leaves, and such a faculty for catching and holding shadows! The quails come quite near; to-day one whistled in our very yard. Sometimes we see them walking about in the short grass. How daintily shy and quaint their movements are!

AUGUST 13.

Another extremely hot day, but so beautiful. In the morning I sat with my work, by a pleasant north window, and felt the joy of being alive. I could hear blue-jays from the wooded hill, and the mocking melody of a cat-bird near by, and all the infinite, lulling tones that rise and pulse on summer air. There was just enough of sunshine to cast the dreamiest of shadows. In such a light, the roughest stone and rudest bit of wood is idealized, like homely and common words breathed in music.

AUGUST 18.

At daybreak a heavy fog, through which the sun, at rising, streamed gloriously. Phyllis called me to look at the dead thorn-tree, which was draped with hundreds of fairy webs, that but for the fog-pearls bedecking would have been almost as viewless as the air. Every dripping leaf twinkled; no precious stone that was not represented in those gems of liquid light.

I think the clouds are more beautiful in dog-days than at any other season.   To-day they rest, — celestial mountains of glistening pearl, serene against the resplendent blue.   They set one dreaming of Olympian heights, and of the gods who live at ease.

Just now I saw a woodchuck looking out from his den among the rocks in the corner of our yard.   He turned his head warily, this way and that, listening

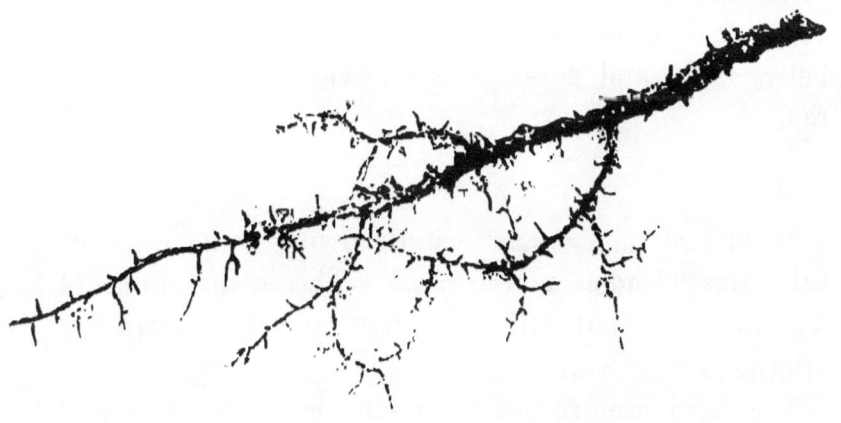

so timidly, as if the sweet air and benignant light were full of unseen arrows.   I spoke, and he slunk back.

Later. — He has made another venture, and at last waxed bold enough to amble across the path.   He looks almost like one of the stones, for he is old and gray. He found what he was after, a sweet apple, and brought it near to his own door, to feel safe in case of surprise.

There he sat upright on his fat haunches, and nibbled voraciously. He uses his forepaws very deftly, turning his apple round and round, as he munches, and then dropping the core in a very human fashion. He has a low, retreating forehead; his muzzle is very dark gray, and his

belly, back, and forelegs are streaked with squirrel-red.

AUGUST 21.

Wild and dark. East wind blowing tremendously; skies like "leaden-colored seas." This in the forenoon. The sun shone out with unwonted splendor before the afternoon was over.

We have been to the grape-vine, at "the old place," and brought home a basketful of the green fruit. We had counted on finding some luscious "bell-pears" on the ground under the old tree; but somebody had foraged before us, and left swinish proof behind them. Tea over, we went outside and sat in the still, cool air. The afterglow of sunset lingered richly in the west, while the south was radiant with the white light of the moon. Katydids are prating raspingly of frost.

Last evening a fitful rain with sudden gusts of wind set in. To-day the storm has developed into a terrific blizzard, from east and south-east. It has broken a large branch out of our pretty door-yard arch of apple-boughs. The pear and butternut trees are broken too. The darkened sky is full of leaves, eddying around, like flocks of frightened birds. The grass is thickly covered with them, and with bits of broken twigs. Apples are lying as thick upon the ground as if the trees had been shaken for a purpose. Our little world looks quite desolate, and Phyllis looks out mournfully on her shattered idols.

Later. — Clouds are breaking, and the blue smiles out serenely, though the gale is still trumpeting. The cardinal-flower that yesterday stood high and dry on the edge of the brook's bed is now wading and bobbing dizzily in the swift current.

More rain and more tempest, followed by a most enchanting evening; moonlit, and warmly alive with a soft rushing in the trees, and voices of crickets, katydids, whip-poor-wills, and the light laughter of the brook.

Very hot; skies a faint lavender-gray, air dreamy blue, sun and shadow delicately blended; strong, southerly breezes.

My tree-toad has moved, and is now keeping house under the wide iron circle that ballasts our well-sweep. We had an excellent opportunity to look at him to-day, through a magnifier. He is very portly, and wears the colors of a dark-gray stone, spotted with light-gray lichen; and if his coat were of silk and velvet, it could not look more elegant. The pouch, where I presume he carries his music, is marked with perfect regularity; tiny seeds of pearl on a dark ground. This morning he came out of his grim round-tower, and resting against its rim and a big nail, sat for some time in the light and air. As the sun-heat increased, he retreated, but chose the hottest part of his roof, wedging himself between that and the wooden beam, where he has since remained. Occasionally he rouses up and lets off one or two trills, whether of dissatisfaction or supreme content, does not appear.

SEPTEMBER.

September 1.

The breeze is dead, a melancholy fine rain falling. The trees are drooping and motionless. Blue-jays' clamoring in the woods is the only sound of cheerful life. Cold shades of leaden gray, are overhead. The earth wears a dejected, blackish green. All the air about the Nunnery seems one plaintive trill of crickets and other insects, all in minor key.

SEPTEMBER 4.

Walked briskly after our late tea. The sky was transparently golden. Against it Cedar Hill made a splendid *silhouette*. Katydid's note was slow and mellow. Crickets never sent up a tenderer hymn. The meadow, the wood, and the shut-in road, though filled with earth's twilight, caught a dim glory from the heavens. The evening star burned near the western horizon, scarcely brighter than the sky. Phyllis was out when I came in, and all the rooms were dark, so I pulled up the window-shades and let in the great east, with its stars and calm, and knew it was better for my soul than any glare or gabble.

SEPTEMBER 5.

The morning is soft and quiet. The dim sunlight, half roseate, paints the world with subdued richness. The sky is not blue, but of a tawny pearl tint, except in the west, where it shows faint shades of violet. The hills are violet too, and the shadows near by are haunted by the same lovely hue.

AFTERNOON.

A few rods to the south the katydids are in a perfect wrangle, two or three trees full. Not one can be heard near the Nunnery. From my walk I brought home a couple of stalks of wild asters and a

few shadowy ferns. I saw a white butterfly sipping
sweets from a white-clover head. A few primrose-
yellow ones went fluttering up and down in happy aim-
lessness, as if intoxicated by mere existence in that

delicious air. I thought no tongue
could tell the beauty, and the something *more* than beauty, that I saw
and felt in that brief walk ; and yet
the words of another came to my
lips, and I said, " Ah, God! Thy
stillness and thy blessedness! The
glory of thy hands, and the gladness of thy sunshine across them! "

SEPTEMBER 6.

Misty, chill, and drear, in the
early hours. Later the clouds
scattered, and the sunbeams, cool
and pale, lit up a very different landscape from yesterday's. It is full of vague melancholy.

SEPTEMBER 7, 4 P.M.

Growing dark. The wind, very wild and warm,
comes from the south. All day I have been more than
usually conscious of space and color. Although I have
been sewing in a corner, with window-shade pulled low,
for the sake of over-sensitive eyes, my inner vision has

been without, in the wide sky, over the swaying woods, roaming at will and believing in heaven, — a real heaven. And I am very happy in an unreasoning sort of way, for to-day perplexities do not perplex. The sphinx is asleep, and has forgotten her riddle.

Chestnut and butternut trees are yellowing. Dull reds show here and there, and red always enchants the eye on a gray-green day like this. The currant-bush on the bank looks as if its tips had been dipped in wine. A tree of red apples leans from the slope at the back of the house. I stood under it to-day and noted the harmony of all. The gray old building, with its one back-chamber window red-curtained, and the red pail on the gray stone step below.

SEPTEMBER 11, Morning.

Bright and cool. A north-east wind is whipping the leaves, which show a cheerless glitter under the white sun. Long lines of grayish-white lie in the south, and little "mare tails" mark the blue of the east and north. The loveliest things in sight to-day are the shadows. The long green lane is alive with their inimitable undulations, and the cool gray of the Nunnery is painted with tossing sprays of a darker and finer gray, such as only nature's "air brush" can create.

SEPTEMBER 15.

A brilliant day. The sun can never be too bright for a wood-ramble, however preferable a clouded sky may seem when one is on the street or out in the open.

This morning as I went over the meadow-slope, before turning into the turfy old cart-path which traverses

the wood, my eyes rejoiced in the lush growth of aftermath, sparkling with dew. Hundreds of grasshoppers went leaping, with a soft crackle of small wings, from before my coming feet. Wild carrot blossoms, on tall, prim stems, shook their heads coldly, as the gay breeze passed with a vain attempt to ruffle their laces.

I paused for a seat on the half-tumbled wall. Gray shadows moved on its lichened stones, keeping time to the wind's rune. At its base were the ferns — beloved ferns! They are no rarity in this locality, but they can never be " common " in a vulgar sense, for they unfailingly give a select and poetic air to every spot where they are found.

A small brown bird from an alder bush cried, " Too weet," and flashed out and away through the bright air. At my right, close by, were the woods, richly green and shining. Above them, in the glowing blue, hovered a pale half-moon — a happy ghost! But the north-west wind blew a trifle chill, so I slipped from my perch and sauntered on, down into the hollow, and crossed a narrow, half-sunken bridge, under which a small stream creeps silently; then up again and round a curve, where, among the rocks, the golden-rod spreads its yellow cheer, and gives freely of its bounty to those bold plunderers, the bees. I stooped to examine one, and quoted to him aloud :

> " O, velvet bee, you're a dusty fellow ;
> You've powdered your legs with gold ! "

but he was too busy delving to heed my impertinence.

A little farther on the trees meet overhead, and through them falls a glorious gloom. Here and there, across my way, were large boughs lying prone as they were hurled by last week's tempest. Some were thick with leaves and full of sap when stricken ; and to these death comes with melancholy slowness. Even the peace-breathing wood has its tragedies.

In the undergrowth that borders the path sumachs crowd and lean, holding stiffly their dark-red clusters, — half-burned torches of smothered fire. A few big, yellow daisies star the thicket shades.

Pale, lilac-gray asters, delicate as any children of the spring, peer out timidly with a look on their unsullied faces that seems one with youth and dawn ; and I am glad that here are ferns for their company : nothing could be fitter.

A flock of blue-jays came darting among the trees, and alighted but a short distance from where I stood, motionless and breathless, to watch them. One proudly crested gallant said, almost softly, " Hullo ! " and one twittered like a robin, and one snarled like a cat-bird. I even fancied there was an attempt to mimic a crow. Some of the birds were of a speckled brown color, and looked demure compared to their celestial-hued brethren, but all were hilarious. To witness such splendid life and exquisite motion is in itself an exhilarant.

SEPTEMBER 16.

Dark and rainy in the morning. Nevertheless I accomplished my little walk, and enjoyed it too, in spite of abundant wet. The world looks autumnal. The soaked hedges are gay with orange, lilac, and brown, and everything green is yellowing except the oaks, which are almost blue by contrast, and the cedars, which take on new vigor as the summer wanes. The taller and coarser ferns are fairly aglow with shades of buff and bright tan.

The wild vine hangs ruddy garlands in the tree, and burns its cool fire in many a sober bush; while the grave-hued walls and fences are wreathed with prodigal crimson.

It is a very gayety of death. As if Nature herself were saying, " To-day we will comfort ourselves with red wine, for to-morrow we die!"

In the afternoon the sun beamed from a blithe heaven. A south wind brought odors from some coal-pit burning in the woods, and with the odors a floating blue vapor that haunted the landscape with a gentle pathos; as if all the sweet ghosts of the innocent trees suffocated in that black pit had met in shadowy concourse, for one last look on beloved haunts, before vanishing into the great ether.

SEPTEMBER 19, 6 A.M.

A quiet, fine rain, dainty as an April shower, is pattering among the leaves. From my opened window I can hear the cheery chickadees and the sweet, short notes of the little brown seed-birds. I can hear a note, too, that resembles a spring peeper's, but whether of bird or frog I know not.

"Singing wings" are drowsy, and make a soft tumult that blends well with the sleepy rain. Distant sounds float clearly and come near: the roar of the train passing on the other side of the woods, and the voices of the road-workers shouting to their team. Clouds are heavy, and lie in long, leaden, wave-shaped lines, changing position but slowly. The asters in the marsh keep their pure color, but look cold on such a morning. Even the sunny golden-rod looks dejected, and all the rusty reds and browns are accentuated. The wooden bridge is blackish-gray; so are many of the stones in the wall. The mosses are there, however, and they never fail to draw fresh life and color from the storm.

Ruskin speaks of mosses as "the lowly faithful," calls them "the first mercy of the earth," and says they lay a "quiet finger on the tumbling stones, to teach them rest."

EVENING.

We have been out with a lamp to interview a katydid that was lustily holding forth just above the entrance of our porch. I was surprised to find him so large, and to see that he was, apparently, creating all that strident clamor by means of a couple of copper-colored cymbals clashing together at the back of his shoulders, being a part of his wings and moved

by them. With every vibration the c r e a t u r e looked like some strange, green, breathing flower, o p e n i n g and s h u t t i n g and opening again. I held the lamp within six inches of his head, but he seemed not abashed by its brightness, a n d continued to assert, in our very faces, that "*Katy certainly did!*"

OCTOBER.

OCTOBER 3, Morning.

When the wan dawn arose, beshrouded and chill, one's faith required help from memory to believe in the living glory hiding "within the veil." Such an hour is not without its deep spiritual significance. Since then the mists have floated up and up, to hang vapory wreaths in the arching blue, while every shining grass-blade holds on its delicate point the sun in miniature. The long-wooded ridge that makes my near horizon seems to pulse and breathe, showing acres upon acres of "twinkling sprays," as the light wind moves among them. With the blue-green of the oaks is mingled now a soft dusk of red that gives a bloomy wild-grape tinge, subtly suggestive of the deep wine glow it will soon become.

Illuminated texts are gleaming in the midst of the maple boughs, and he who runs may read. Trees are always and everywhere lovable, but in their native temple, with only the wild life of nature around them, they are worshipful.

The sparkling air holds a transparent gold, as if it had absorbed somewhat of the spiritual pale yellow of the landscape ; and it holds something more, — a spirit of serenest waiting, of cheerful leisure and content. It is sweet Life facing great Death, and facing him with unclouded glance and unquestioning tranquillity. It is like an angel's presence, and fills the soul with a divine hope and gladness.

Every day, and more and more, I am astonished at the blind ignorance of most of us concerning the ways and the laws of the out-of-door world and its myriad lives. I am mortified in the presence of so many unsolved conundrums! Yesterday I *saw*, for the first time, how a common field-cricket sings, and I venture to say that my personal observation of

the subject was on a par with most of my neighbors'.

A few weeks ago our well became temporarily dry,
and we made the bucket stationary on the stonework
inside the curb. This poised the heavy end of the

sweep between one and two feet from the ground.
Some time after (it may have been days or weeks) I
noticed depending from this same beam end something
that, at first glance, looked like a very coarse, dull
fringe. The strands, which were as large as a pipe-stem,
were an inch or so apart, and five or six inches long, and
all arranged with the utmost precision. Instead of
standing reverently before this miracle, my idle curios-
ity put out a careless hand, and with one little brush

sent the whole frail wonder to destruction. Then I dis-
covered that each strand was a kind of dry hanging
well, walled with grains of earth and holding countless
pale, naked mites that wriggled feebly as they tried to
extricate themselves from the ruins. If I had been a
genuine tornado I couldn't have felt meaner. And ever
since I have wondered over those buildings and their
builder. How were those grains of earth persuaded to
hold so lightly together in the face of wind and damp
and the law of gravitation?

OCTOBER 6.

The pale ferns have a vanishing look, and appear to
mingle more and more, daily, with the mists and
shadows, as well as the impalpable fine gold of sunnier
air. Up among the cedars, where we walked to-day,
we saw such clouds of them. And O, such a splendor
of color everywhere! "Banners yellow, glorious,
golden;" yea, crimson, scarlet, and even pink. The
sweet-fern patches are dark greenish-purple; huckleberry leaves are deep, warm red. Beds of everlasting,
silvery and cool, stand side by side with tulip gayety.
The fine, bleached grass on the hill-slope is silken to
the foot, and looks like an aureole of mist. Among the
cedars there is one pine-tree. It is fast turning gray,
and shaking down its hoary locks with every gust.

OCTOBER 9.

From my pillow, early this morning, I saw through the bare, still boughs of the apple-tree near my window the divine peace of gold-gray heavens. The dawn always comes as a fresh miracle, and fills the soul with adoring awe. A thin violet haze hung in the air, and when the sun looked over the horizon rim, long, divergent rays shot through the purple, and caught the old chest-nut-tree at the end of the lane, clothing it with a nimbus. The breeze has awakened now, and with every touch sends loosened leaves flickering away through "shadow and shine," — brown and yellow wings that beat lightly among the twigs as they go to be harbored at last on the great earth-breast, — "Frail, wind-tossed voyagers on the tide of time." Why does not some artist picture the flight of the leaves? It might be almost as lovely as the "Flight of the birds."

Speaking of birds, there is a flock of those inimitable blue-jays frolicking together across the way. They keep up a soft, sociable twitter, that I am sure must be a sort of conversation, — words that my dull ear covets to understand.

OCTOBER 15.

Very cool, with brisk breezes and a brilliant sky. Many trees are quite denuded, and expose beautiful dark-gray twigs and boughs. Swamp maples, butternuts, and chestnuts are among the first to "let the truthful sunlight through."

From my window I can no longer distinguish the ferns ; but the morning light sheds glory even in their loved and vacant places, now so brown and sere.

OCTOBER 17.

Twilight afterglow. The sun is gone, but has left an overflowing heaven of sweetest light. How exquisitely delicate is the amber fringe of white birches against the sky! The woods and fields look consciously blessed. I noted to-day, while out, that the half-blackened torch of the sumach had lost its candelabra of gorgeous leaf-age ; only the framework of smooth-branching stems remains. Our one lofty white-wood tree never looked more kingly. It, too, is bereft of leaves : the clearly outlined seed-tips all stand erect and graceful, in per-fect accord with the stately and dignified character of the tree.

OCTOBER 21.

Sunny and warm, albeit a little searching breeze hails from the east. This morning I sat and listened to the sunrise sounds. The cawing of crows, and the scream-ing of jays in the woods, the barking of a distant dog, the crowing of cocks, the lowing of unseen cattle, and the voice of an invisible man calling "co boss ! co boss !"

Nearer, a squirrel's bright chatter and a chickadee's blithe singing.

The occasional report of a shot-gun was the only discordant note in the whole pastoral symphony.

The brooding sky is curtained by low-hanging clouds. The woods are damp and tattered, but still hold much of brightness. The myriad fluttering, wet pennants on the white birches are almost as brilliant as buttercups. I can never sufficiently admire these slender, swaying, white-bodied trees, growing so profusely on the wooded ridge opposite my window. The oaks, "with soul of might," and the cedars' green repose, give strength and richness of tone; but the general background of color in the woods is a soft purplish-brown, crossed and recrossed by dim gray stems.

OCTOBER 23.

Pleasantly warm in spite of a driving rain from the east. The brook that has been shrinking and silent of late is rising fast, and will soon sing from a full heart.

OCTOBER 24.

A day of silvery mists, and sunshine falling from a pale, far sky; the softest of airs and the lulling sound of full-flowing streams. The odor of wet moss and decaying leaves is delightfully strong. When I shut my eyes to the tags of bright color, clinging to the landscape, and ignore the mat of long, green autumn grass, I could easily fancy this to be a spring day. There is even a peeper contributing his mite of shrill piping to complete the illusion.

EVENING.

A vast, moon-rayed phantom of fog looms solemnly between earth and sky; yet the katydid's debate is in nowise damped or hindered, and the ground crickets are merry.

OCTOBER 25, Morning.

A wholesome breeze has puffed the fog into a great bank southward, leaving the northern sky luminously clear. The sunrise was flame color, and burned behind the woody crown of the hill like clear fire. The moving of boughs before it made the semblance perfect.

How dear and beautiful it all is! Who can help loving the lithe, bare stems and rugged boles, the wind-blown flocks of changing leaves, the zigzag ramble of ancient fence and venerable wall, and over these, and more than all, the measureless deeps of tinted air, that bathe the soul as with a tide of melody?

NOVEMBER.

NOVEMBER 30.

We have always heard of "drear November." It is called the month of wailing, and is often used as a symbol of despairing woe ; but to me its personality is as soothing as might be the presence of a strong-hearted, serene-faced Quaker of ripe, middle age and rich experience, clothed, as it is, in unobtrusive grays and browns ; loving stillness and the unhindered rays of the truthful sun, yet all undaunted by the dark tumult of passing storms.

If all the bright leaves, like so many rainbow hopes, are fallen, they yet make, like pleasant memories, a warmth and sober brightness ; while the denuded trees, having laid aside every burden, are all the better fitted for wrestling with the elements.

The pale mornings glisten with films of frost, idealizing and refining every feature of the land, even as the human face is softened by a crown of silvered hair.

The skies wear a far-away, half-veiled, ineffable expression. Some of us have seen that look in beloved eyes, that were already beholding, dimly yet rapturously, " the heaven-side bank of the river of Death." It is the forerunner of " that divinely transfigured sleep, as of victory," in whose majestic presence we can neither strive nor cry for the deep peace at its heart.

To-day has been " Thanksgiving." We have been talking a good deal, in a quiet way, about other Thanksgiving days, when those we loved, as we can never love aught again, were with us in warm and joyous flesh· *Now* our little table is set for but two.

From Prospect Heights, five miles away, we could

faintly hear a wavering melody. It came from old
Trinity's bell, whose deep tone, etherealized by distance

and its passage over dale and hill, seemed to add a
hallowing charm to the fresh and tranquil air. To us
it suggested organ anthems, and dim aisles, fragrant

with the breath of snow-white chrysanthemums, or
" Christ flowers," as they are sometimes called. The
day has seemed a sort of *holy* day, and we have felt like
putting common cares aside.

Phyllis gave me a mild start by saying abruptly, " I
am going to have a fernery ! " I said, " Yes — but how ?"
Her reply was somewhat incoherent, and supplemented
by a hasty putting on of wraps and rubbers, and the
next moment she was out of doors, making a rapid bee-
line for the woods. Phyllis is subject to sudden inspi-
rations. In half an hour she had returned, rosy and
animated from her eager quest, with arms full of moss
and up-rooted ferns, to which great lumps of rich, black
leaf-mould clung heavily, giving out subtle and penetrating odors. " Oh," she said, breathlessly, " do smell
them ! Aren't they delicious ? — and the day is so
lovely. I felt like a child while out; the air is like
spring, and the woods seemed alive with memories."
There were bronze-green club mosses, and pale-gray
" tree " mosses, and the ferns were of the dark, tiny-
plumed variety, such as flourish nowhere better than in
our own deep well.

All this time the fernery was to my mind but a vague
possibility, yet having great faith in Phyllis' resources
I waited hopefully while she went on a rummage in the
garret. It was a simple arrangement after all, just an
oval wooden platform and a glass dome to fit, that had
formerly been used for a basket of wax flowers. A

glass dish with a substratum of gravel and charcoal, then the earth, with its wiry rootlets carefully disposed and the mosses arranged comfortably; a generous sprinkling of lukewarm water, and, presto! the fernery had become a visible fact.

True, it is small, less than a foot in diameter, but it is a world by itself. Day by day a mist will rise from the moist earth and gather on the glass, to duly fall again and keep the bits of wild life fresh and sparkling; and it will be a joy through all the winter months to us, who may not keep " house plants " in the often rigorous atmosphere of the Nunnery.

DECEMBER.

DECEMBER 15.

We have had a call to-day from a rare young woman whose circle in life is far removed from our own. She is city born and bred, — culture, education, soft manners, all are hers. In addition she has a genuine love for the country, even in its most bleak and forbidding aspect, and doesn't mind being called a storm " tramp," often walking miles in the face of rain or sleet. This latter quality makes a bit of common ground on which I can meet her easily, in spite of the shyness I invariably feel in the presence of such bright youthfulness.

I like to recall the picture she made as she looked

back from the windy street, with cap uplifted and the tempest in her hair. She is like Emily Dickinson's "Purple Clover:"

> "She doth not wait for June;
> Before the world is green
> Her sturdy little countenance
> Against the wind is seen."

CHRISTMAS EVE.

In my lap lies my one lovely, unlooked-for gift from a far-away friend, Bryant's "Library of Poetry and Song." Phyllis smiles approval when I tell her I shall say my prayers to Santa Claus this night.

Within these solid covers I have been renewing intimacy with many an old favorite, cherished in days gone by, but lost sight of in my wanderings.

They meet me now like noble friends, after long absence and many changes.

DECEMBER 31.

> "Grand is the leisure of the earth!
> She gives her happy myriads birth,
> And, after harvest, fears not death,
> But goes to sleep in snow-wreaths dim,"

while we her children become joyful inheritors.

Now in these brief days and long nights, how grateful is the glow of one's own hearth-fire!

The evening lamp points to beloved volumes, and

beckons us to high thoughts and transcendent company.
But we will leave our curtains open for the winter stars
to look in, and we shall read no poems like

> " That old measure in the boughs,
>   That phraseless melody

> " The wind does, working like a hand
>   Whose fingers brush the sky,
>   Then quiver down with tufts of tune
>   Permitted gods and me."

www.ingramcontent.com/pod-product-compliance
Lightning Source LLC
Chambersburg PA
CBHW020804020726
47495CB00008B/2577